THE WATER OF LIFE REMAINS IN THE DEAD

Maria Nieto

FLORICANTO PRESS

FLORICANTO™ PRESS

7177 Walnut Canyon Rd.

Moorpark, California 93021

(415) 793-2662

www. FLORICANTOPRESS. com

ISBN-13: 978-1519146182

Cover Art *The Grieving: Ciudad Juárez 2004* by Rebekah Tarín (brushfireartemasfina.com, brushfire575@gmail.com)

"Por nuestra cultura hablarán nuestros libros. Our books shall speak for our culture."

Roberto Cabello-Argandoña and Leyla Namazie, Editors

WATER OF LIFE

ACKNOWLEDGMENTS

I am honored that the talented artist, Rebekah Tarín, gave permission to use the image of her painting entitled, *The Grieving: Ciudad Juarez 2004*, for the book's cover. As I have worked to do with this story, Rebekah's art forces us to see the unseen; the victims we never knew, those killed under the cover of nightfall. The adventures of Alejandra Marisol, the protagonist in this story, came to life with the support of so many. I am grateful to my mom, Caroline Aguirre, Rebecca Carrillo, Irma Castruita, Helen Garfinkle, Electra Flink, Jane Armbruster, Karen Choury, and my aunts, Helen (Varmint) Nájera and Virginia Andrade, for their willingness to read an early draft of the work. Their feedback was instrumental to keep me in the writing trenches when the negative voices tried to drag down my spirit. Gratitude goes out to Terry Cunningham, Jane Barbarow, and Lucha Corpi, who provided detailed edits following multiple readings of the work. They were tough, pushing me to let go of text that was strangling the pace of the story. The quality of the wording and storyline were vastly improved with their input and I am indebted for their generous gift of time and commitment. I am deeply thankful to former LAPD detective (Robbery-Homicide Division), William Williams. William's knowledge of LAPD procedures and tactics, in addition to his expertise in American history, proved invaluable in the research phases of this work. I would also like to thank Jennifer Brody for allowing me to share a personal memory that I used in this book. Over the course of three years to write this story, Jennifer Vásquez was there to listen to half-baked ideas, offer advice, and provide loving, daily support. I am lucky and thankful to be on this journey with her. Finally, I thank my publisher at Floricanto Press, Roberto Cabello-Argandoña, and editor, Leyla Namazie, for their commitment to Latino stories and voices.

Chapter 1

NO BED OF ROSES

Hell did not encircle a wretched pit beneath layers of molten earth. No, from where I stood, it was located in East Los Angeles at the southern edge of Belvedere Park. There I could see the outline of the devil's playground; five murdered men whose bodies showed the signs of Detective Ashworth's sadistic handiwork. How was it possible? I had seen Ashworth writhe in pain and take his last breath. He had confessed to everything before swallowing the cyanide capsule, and from all accounts these latest murders occurred after his death.

I felt a tug at my arm. "This is a restricted area, Miss. You'll need to leave."

"My name is Alejandra Marisol. I'm a reporter for the *Los Angeles Times*."

"Leave her be, Deputy." I turned to find Lieutenant Smitz towering over me. He no longer intimidated me unlike the first time we met. I had gone to see the high ranked sheriff to inquire about two unsolved murders. Days later I learned the victims died at the hands of John Ashworth. "Miss Marisol, I didn't think you'd want to see me again," He said with a sarcastic tone.

"Seems that bourbon, or is it the Scotch you drink each night is pickling your brain."

"What gave you the idea I might have a drink from time to time?"

"It's all over your face. And the liquor lines tell me from time to time, really means all of the time with you."

"Ah, a little spitfire. What's it been, a week since we first met? You've grown some backbone."

"One doesn't almost get killed, not once but several times, witness unspeakable horrors, and not get affected by it."

"Seems you'd understand my indulgences then, which by the way, favor the taste of Tennessee Whiskey, straight up, no rocks."

"Drinking, okay, I get it. You have a tough job. But I'll never understand your penchant to hurt me, and others like me, all out of pure contempt. You're a racist bigot, plain and simple."

"What makes you think you can talk to me like that and still get what you want, a closer look at the crime scene for your story?"

I took a breath. I had never felt so strong and in control. "Look, I'm tied to this hell, which I thought ended when Detective Ashworth died and his Los Angeles Police Department accomplices were arrested. But now there's a truck with five bodies, and it's going to catch headlines. People will want answers."

"Ashworth was LAPD, my department wasn't involved."

"Right. Your Sheriff's Department is above the fray for now. If the investigation determines these murders are tied to a child sex trade operation and that one of your kind orchestrated it, the public won't care if it's a Sheriff or an LAPD cop who's to blame."

Smitz turned away. He drew his right hand up to his forehead and slowly pulled his hand across and down his crew cut hairline. He turned back toward me and I could see the look of surrender in his face. He motioned for me to follow as he led the way toward a bloodstained white pickup truck.

There was no sanity in what I saw. Each man had been butchered. Slaughtered was the right word. Their eyes stared at me, begging me to know their slow and painful death.

In a voice wrenched with defeat Smitz spoke, "It's a horror show."

Smitz's words didn't even begin to tell the story. Some say the moment we die our soul is unchained and the pain of life that dug its claws into our flesh ceases. Suffering ends, furrows fade, and the face of youth reappears. I saw no such face among these men. I saw a fate no one should come to know. I focused on one man; he was young. Like the other victims he had been skinned with an arm torn off. His eyes bulged. His mouth locked open. I could imagine his screams; a relentless torment that raged until he was freed from this world. I kept my eyes on him, hoping my stare could change the scene or make it go away. The pungent odor of oxidized iron from the pools and spatter of blood covering the truck's bed confirmed I couldn't change a thing.

I turned away from the grisly scene. "Who will be the detective on the case?"

"Leighton Carr. I'll introduce you."

Smitz called out to Carr who stood at the front end of the truck jotting notes. "Detective Carr."

Carr was short and stout, and the grey suit jacket reaching down to his knees made him appear compressed. "Smitz, you old man. Why the formality?"

"There's someone I want you to meet. This is Alejandra Marisol. I think you'll find her a good resource for your case."

Detective Carr gave me a sideways glance and directed his attention to Smitz. "So tell me how this woman is going to help?"

"There's a good chance these bodies are tied to Detective Ashworth out of LAPD, the one who took his life the other night. Alejandra was working with him, investigating a sex ring. She didn't know Ashworth ran the sick operation, but in the end she was the one who brought him down."

"So you're telling me Miss Marisol was duped by Ashworth and happened to be lucky enough to get out of a pretty dangerous spot. There's no way she's going to be part of this investigation, no way in hell. Anyway, I'm steps ahead of her. Just saw Ashworth's body at the morgue and after I leave here I'm heading to his house."

"I know what you're thinking Carr, I thought the same thing, but the girl's got fire in her belly. Why limit your resources? She may have insights into Ashworth that can help with the case."

I cut in, "Ashworth wasn't just operating a sex ring; it was a child sex trade and I was deep into the investigation."

Carr questioned, "Investigation? Where do you work?"

"I'm a reporter with the *Times*."

"Oh no, Smitz. You can't be serious. You want me to work with a reporter?"

"She's got info on this case that hasn't even been penned to a report. She knows stuff."

"But I can't officially let her take part in this investigation. You know that."

I answered for Smitz. "Unofficially, you can. Look, you're going to Ashworth's home, let me go with you."

An exasperated Carr responded. "Damn it, woman, you're not going."

Smitz complied, "Okay, Carr has the final word on

this. I won't pull rank. Homicide detectives call the shots on the murders."

Carr smirked in my direction. He turned and walked away.

My jaw clamped and I could feel the heat rise in my face, but I stayed calm. One way or another I'd get inside Ashworth's house.

Chapter 2

HOUSE CALL

I had what I needed for my assignment. I could return to the *Times* Building, write the initial report on these murders, and end my part in it. But my gut told me the macabre scene was tied to someone other than Ashworth. Someone who wanted to send a message: a warning that a cruel and painful death awaited me or anyone else who wanted to dig for the truth. The danger signs were clearly posted, but I didn't care. I was ready for battle.

I sat in *Azulita,* my blue VW Beetle, and stared in the rearview mirror at my blank canvas, a pair of pale bow shaped lips. I grabbed my war paint: a tube of Revlon lipstick color number 703. "Brazen Bliss," the cosmetic company's top selling color for women with caramel brown skin like mine was my talisman of late; it unleashed a fire inside. With the precision of a portrait painter I set to work. I started at one end by applying subtle pressure as I spread the rich red and tawny tones across my bottom lip to the opposite corner of my mouth. I then used the tip of my tool to outline the top of my canvas before filling it in with color.

Waiting for Carr to finish his work at the crime scene, I knew I needed to summon all the strength, imagined or real I could get.

I kept my eyes on Carr and watched as he got into his dark brown sedan and drove off. I followed him into Pasadena as he wound his way up Lake Avenue beneath the shadow of Echo Mountain to turn down a tree-lined street in Altadena. Carr stopped behind a patrol car parked in the driveway of a nondescript single level home. I kept my distance and pulled against the curb three houses away.

In less than an hour, Carr and two patrol deputies left. I made my way down a long driveway to the rear of the house. I tried my luck with the sliding glass patio door, but no go; it was locked. I noticed the other side of the house was out of public view, shielded by a high concrete wall and an overgrown oleander bush. After pushing through the shrubbery, I found a small bathroom window ajar. With my hands pressed against the house and legs pushed up against the back wall, I inched upward. I strained to hold position and used my right hand to push the window open. I propelled forward and nearly landed head first into the toilet bowl as I hit the ground.

Sore from the impact I moved slowly to stand. The

bathroom was unremarkable. A single towel hung over a hook on the wall and the standard items sat on a shelf above the sink: shaving cream, razor, and cologne.

Ashworth's bedroom was my next stop. There I found a scene of meticulous order. A lone chest of drawers alongside a bed that could easily pass a drill sergeant's inspection sat centered against one wall. I opened each drawer to find perfect rows of t-shirts, socks and underwear, all folded as if on display at a high-end department store. Ashworth's closet mirrored the same attention to detail. Jackets and slacks were neatly hung and organized by color. Shoes were aligned on the floor and fitted with shoehorns.

I walked to the living room where a drab beige chair and sofa sat against an eggshell painted wall. The only color in the room came from a lone painting of a small boat tied alongside a riverbank. The place reminded me of a hospital waiting room. I turned to find a small desk and chair at the other end of the room. A framed photograph sat on the desk; the only personal effect in the entire house. It pictured Ashworth standing with an attractive woman and two small children. I presumed the woman was one of his ex-wives. Everyone in the picture smiled; they looked happy. The image of Ashworth was in sharp contrast to the psychopath I came to know: a cold and calculating killer.

I searched the rest of the house and came up empty. Maybe Carr had found something and taken it with him? I had my doubts. I looked back at the photo with Ashworth. "What are you still hiding, you madman?"

The photo didn't fit the space. I was curious to see if there was a year written on it. I removed the frame's backing and there behind the picture were the names John, Shirley, Katie and John Jr. with the year 1960 written underneath. As I replaced the happy family portrait in the frame the cardboard insert slipped and three weathered Polaroid photos fell free. In the first one, I immediately identified a younger Ashworth dressed in his LAPD patrol uniform. He was standing with other officers whom I recognized as well. They were the same men, his child sex trade accomplices, who had tried to kill us. But one man in the picture, also dressed in his LAPD "blues", I didn't recognize.

The next photograph pictured an older man with a look of shock running across his face as the camera caught him in bed with a much younger woman. I moved to the last photo. It pictured a younger man with a naked woman tied to the bed. The woman's head was turned to the side; her eyes avoided the camera's lens. The man on top of her looked smug and angry.

I wondered if these photos represented Ashworth's start in photography before he began taking pictures of the kids he intended to sell for sex. In comparison to Ashworth's work using younger subjects these photos were benign. Nevertheless, I wanted to find out if they were somehow tied to the five murdered men.

Chapter 3

MAKING BONES ABOUT IT

Even though I had met him less than a week ago, my heart pumped at full speed for Dr. Armand Gomez. I felt no need to put on the brakes. I was ready to enjoy the ride wherever it took me. Armand's call rocked me out of bed, and in a matter of minutes I dressed and left to meet him at the morgue. He had worked through the night conducting autopsies on the five dead men.

When I arrived I found Armand placing a heart in a large open scale. "Alejandra, good to see you. Let me get the weight on this and I'll be right with you. They just brought this guy in about an hour ago. Looks like he died of a heart attack in his sleep, but since he was found on the street he became a coroner's case."

"The work never ends for you, does it?"

"You're right, death is the one thing I count on, or rather counts on me, everyday."

Armand removed his gloves and moved in closer. "I'd sure like to count on something else."

He raised his hand to my face and gently brushed my cheek. In one smooth, uninterrupted move he placed his head into the crook of my neck. I felt his long curls as he paused to breathe in my smell. I wanted nothing more than to feel his full lips on my skin. "You've got me spinning, Alejandra. I'd love to be able to count on seeing you."

I could barely say the words. "I'd like that."

"You just made my day. Now, I guess we should focus on those victims for you. Come on over, I think you'll be pleased with what I have so far."

Armand grabbed his notes. "First, looks like the victims spent some time in cold storage after they were killed so I can't give you an exact time of death."

"But from what I saw it seemed as if all five men were massacred in the bed of the truck. It didn't look like the bodies had been moved there."

"Detective Carr had the same idea. He thinks maybe someone drove the truck into some sort of cold storage warehouse."

"Armand, they must have been stored close by. Who would risk driving through the streets of L.A. with bloodied bodies in the back of a truck?"

Armand concurred. "You've got a point."

"Since the bodies were in cold storage that means Ashworth could have killed them before he died."

"I wouldn't be able to rule out that possibility."

"What else do you have?"

"All of the men bled to death after their arms were torn off. There were no tattoos or scars, which may have told us something about their identity. One of the men, approximate age 55, showed lung damage; the air sacs were inflamed and there was scar tissue. I'm running some tests to see if I can tell what caused it. The other four men appear to be much younger. I'd say about 20 years of age."

"How did you figure out the ages?"

"I look at the ribs of the sternum. The integrity at the end of a rib can tell you a lot."

"That's amazing, but I wish we had names."

"I might have a partial name for the older victim. ED, maybe short for Eduardo, is stamped into the victim's leather belt. After I found small pieces of leather under the victim's index fingernail I re-examined the belt. Not sure what it means, but it looks like the victim etched five numbers into the leather. Maybe he was trying to leave a clue knowing he was about to die."

"Can I take a look?"

"Sure, here it is. The numbers follow his name."

I questioned, "But what could five numbers mean? You need seven for a phone number. Could it be part of an address?"

"I don't know, but there's more. Although the left arm on the body has been removed, I'm certain the hands from both arms were tied pretty tight at one point. Look here, below the wrist. Bruising and lacerations indicate he must have been bound with a coarse rope. The deepest laceration is on the radius side of the arm. It indicates the victim made an effort to etch the numbers in such a way they'd follow his name on the side of the belt. Not sure why he didn't just etch the numbers, where he'd have greatest access and ease, on the stretch of leather running across his back."

"Looks as if he may have been interrupted too. Even though I can tell this last number is a three, it's not complete. I'm guessing if he had more time he would have etched in a full phone number."

Armand responded with anticipation in his voice. "I

think we'll know more after my cousin, Olivia, runs some tests."

"Olivia?"

"She's a biochemist, a real genius. She's always inventing something in her laboratory at Caltech. I tell her about my cases and sometimes she can help. She'll be here any minute to pick up some samples."

"What kind of samples?"

"Teeth and bone. Ah, there she is now."

I turned to see a middle-aged woman with short, wiry gray hair. I immediately saw the family resemblance. Like Armand she had deep dimples bordering the corners of her lips, and her eyes were warm and embracing. With the eagerness and energy of a schoolgirl she greeted Armand.

"¡*Hola, Primo*! How's my baby cousin? Knee deep in blood today?"

Armand walked over to give his cousin a big hug and then turned toward me. "Olivia, this is Alejandra."

"Good to meet you. I'm happy to see my cousin spending time with a beautiful woman who's still in possession of her soul, unlike the bodies lining the halls in here."

I was immediately taken with Olivia's charm much like the day I met Armand. "Nice to meet you, Olivia. I hear you might be able to shed some light on the case."

"Well I hope so. Armand gives me a chance to put my experimentation to good use, and with the samples he'll give me I should be able to determine where the victims have been living over the last few years and where they were born."

Anxiously I asked, "How can you do that?"

"Science lifts the fog so one can see."

I questioned Olivia again, "But how?"

"We are what we drink, and the water we drink comes from the rain that falls around us. The water molecules in rain contain oxygen, and inside the nucleus of most oxygen atoms there are 16 small sub-atomic particles. Hence, we call it oxygen 16 or write it like this."

Olivia wrote the notation ^{16}O on paper for me to see and then continued. "Oxygen 16 makes up most of the oxygen found in water. Although less abundant in comparison, water also contains other types of oxygen atoms that have more sub-atomic particles and are therefore heavier, like oxygen 18. An easy way to look at it is to see that every glass of water we drink mostly contains oxygen 16, but a bit of oxygen 18 will be there too. Here's where it gets really interesting. The ratio of oxygen 18 to oxygen 16 found in rainwater naturally varies from one geographic location to another."

I piped in, "I think I see where you're going."

"You got it, Honey. I will be able to determine the ratio of oxygen 18 to oxygen 16 in the teeth and bone of each victim. Once I have the ratios I'll compare them to known values for rainwater across geographic areas. Since most teeth are formed by childhood, determining the ratio for this tissue will tell me where the person was born or at least where they spent their early childhood years. On the other hand, because new bone tissue gets made over time, determining the ratio for this sample type will tell me where the person lived over the last few years. So you see, as sure as a rock turns to dust, the water of life remains in the dead."

Armand couldn't contain his pride. "Isn't she brilliant?"

I couldn't hold back either. "This is incredible."

Olivia agreed, "Yes, quite incredible. Armand go ahead and give me the samples and I'll get to work as soon as I get back to the lab."

With the samples in hand Olivia approached me. "It was so nice to meet you. Off I go."

"I'd better go too."

"Not so fast, Alejandra. You're forgetting about Ashworth's body."

"I assumed there'd be nothing to tell me other than what I already knew. He died from cyanide poisoning."

"Did you know about the wolf tattoo on Ashworth's arm?"

Armand's question had recalled an image I would never forget. When I first saw the photo of a man sexually violating a screaming child, I had no idea it was Ashworth. The photo had been ripped and Ashworth's face had been torn away. But the arm with a wolf tattoo, the one he used to restrain a child, was clearly visible. Ashworth had savagely killed people to get that photograph back in his possession, and he had come close to killing me for it, too.

I answered Armand with a cool voice. "I know about it. If there's a devil, then Ashworth is his name. Do me a favor, when you see Detective Carr don't tell him I was here?"

"Your secret is safe with me."

"Thanks. Will I see you later?"

Armand responded with a smile. "You can count on it."

When I returned to the morgue reception I recognized the woman in the photograph with Ashworth. It was his ex-wife. She stood with an older man. I slowed to hear her conversation with the receptionist.

"I'm here to claim a body."

"The mortuary should be able to handle that for you, Ma'am."

"Yes, they should be here any minute. I wanted to oversee the process. My daughter asked me to."

"Name of the deceased?"

"John Ashworth."

"Your name?"

"Shirley James."

"Relation?"

"I'm his ex-wife."

"Please have a seat."

The likeness was clear. Shirley James was the woman pictured in the family portrait with Ashworth. Why was she here? The look on her face suggested she wasn't just here for her daughter. Her eyes told me at one time she loved John Ashworth. Maybe she never stopped? How did a vile man get a beautiful woman to love him? Another example of how life makes no sense; no sense at all.

Chapter 4
IT'S ALL IN THE EYES

Large fans set off a collective rattle as their metal caged heads oscillated from side to side; the loud din muted the sound of typing in the newsroom. As expected, Harriett's editorial office rivaled the Los Angeles skyline with its thick layer of hovering haze.

"How can you breathe in here?" I asked.

"Light one up. I guarantee you won't notice the smoke anymore. Plus, after what we just went through barely escaping with our lives; these little babies keep me from losing my last nerve."

In a rare sight Harriett's greying blond hair wasn't snared in a bun. Her thick locks fell onto the shoulders of a tailored pantsuit. She tapped out another cigarette from her pack and lit it using a smoldering butt. "Did you learn anything from the crime scene? I thought I would have heard from you yesterday."

"I guess I expected to see you at Rocky's."

"Right, you live in the same fourplex. Rocky decided to come to my place and make me dinner. Said I needed a good home-cooked meal."

"Yeah, I noticed he didn't make it home last night."

"Keeping tabs on him, eh?"

"Only with the best intentions. He's like my dad."

"Yes, he told me he thinks of you like a daughter." Harriett got right back to business. "So what do you have?"

"As you already know there were five men murdered. None of them had ID. The medical examiner, Armand Gomez, was able to get a rough idea of their ages by examining their ribs. I should know more after Armand's cousin runs some tests. She's a scientist from Caltech and she thinks she'll be able to determine where they were born and where they've been living over the last few years."

"How's that possible?"

"It's a long story, but when Armand gives me the results I'll let you know."

"Armand, huh. First name basis, I see things are going well with the doctor."

"Uh..."

"No need to get flustered, you're not the only one who found love through this hell with Ashworth. Anything else on the murders?"

"The investigating officer on the case, Detective Carr, is not cooperating. I followed him to Ashworth's house though. When he left I managed to make my way inside and found these."

I threw the three photographs onto Harriett's desk.

"What do we have here?"

"Look at the first one. There's Ashworth when he was an LAPD patrol officer. I recognize all of the others with him, except for the one on the end."

Harriett agreed, "Yes, I recognize all of these monsters too. The men who were bent on killing me, all of us. The man on the end, I don't recognize either."

"I need to find out who he is. Any ideas?"

"I have a good contact at LAPD's Internal Affairs Division. If he was LAPD then Captain Allen should be able to help identify him. I'll call the captain before you leave and ask him if he has time to see you."

"That'd be great."

Harriett picked up the next photo. "Damn. This is

Judge Thomas. Ha, I can't say I'm surprised."

"What do you know about him?"

"Important man, a judge for the superior court with aspirations for a seat on the Supreme Court of California. He would have paid dearly to keep this photo from reaching the press."

"I guess I'll have to pay him a visit and ask."

"That's not possible. He died a couple months back. If I remember correctly, it was a heart attack at 90."

"Literally, that's a dead end."

Harriett moved on to the last photo. "Looks like this guy was also caught with his pants down. Don't know who he is, but his eyes strike me as familiar."

"Do you think he could be some sort of public figure?"

"Hell, I don't know, but I'd guess there's a strong possibility since his photo was found with the one of Judge Thomas. I'll bet Judge Thomas and this other man were being blackmailed. Alejandra, do you think we're still in danger? Whoever killed those five men may want to come after us, too."

"I think if they wanted to come after us they would have already done so. I think the five men were killed to tie up loose ends. Killing us would only make a mess of things."

"Did Dr. Gomez, oh, I mean Armand, give you an estimate on time of death?"

"He can't, not exactly. Looks like the bodies spent some time in cold storage."

"Wouldn't that mean Ashworth could be responsible?"

"I'm sure that's what Detective Carr thinks, and he'll use it to close the case."

"And I gather from your response you don't think Ashworth committed these murders."

"I don't. In my gut I know this doesn't end with Ashworth; it only begins with him. Right now, I just need the time to prove it."

"Well, Girl, you're tenacious I'll give you that. I'll support you on my end as long as I can. You won't have a lot of time. Once Carr closes the case there will be pressure on the paper to follow in short order."

"Why?"

"The public won't like the idea that murdering sexual predators are on the loose. The paper will give the public what it wants: a nicely wrapped package tied with a pretty bow."

"Even if that package is carrying lies?"

"I've been around a long time and from my editorial vantage point the public has proven one thing over and over: they love their Pablum. This paper is happy to comply and spoon feed it."

"Well, I don't like Pablum. I prefer a plate of spicy jalapeños. I'll keep you posted on what I turn up."

"Be careful, Alejandra. Oh, and try not to break the law. The police and this paper won't stand idly by if you're caught breaking into someone's house."

"Got it."

Chapter 5

MAN IN BLUE

Captain Allen assured Harriett he could help identify the man in the photograph, assuming he was an LAPD police officer. As the head of the Internal Affairs Division, Harriett told me the captain had access to information on every officer. It didn't take long for me to walk from the *Times* building over to Parker Center; a sleek edifice with an exterior made of glass and white stone on Los Angeles Street. You didn't have to look twice to see how LAPD's administration building earned the nickname "Glass House."

When I arrived at Captain Allen's office on the sixth floor, a cherub faced man dressed in a tailored uniform greeted me with a smile. He reached out both of his hands and I instinctively held out mine to meet him in a warm clasp.

"Welcome, Alejandra. Harriett told me to expect you. Sorry to hear about your awful run in with John Ashworth. Even though I'm coming into this a bit late, I want to do anything I can to help. I wish we could have stopped him before he was able to hurt so many."

"Happy to be here. Any help I can get would be great."

Captain Allen chuckled, "Ha, there aren't many who are happy to be here. Internal Affairs or IAD as we call it isn't a favorite. No matter, I like what I do. It's important to have watchdogs out there. And still some, like Ashworth, get through the cracks."

Captain Allen took a seat and motioned for me to do the same. "You know Alejandra, I can't help but think that many of the problems within our department stem from the days when Chief Parker held the reins. Parker's 'Thin Blue Line' played like a perpetual Disneyland ticket for rogue cops to ride their patrol cars and do as they pleased."

"What's the 'Thin Blue Line'?"

"Parker's strategy to decrease the number of beat officers on the street. And, in their place, increase the number of officers in patrol cars. Parker thought less contact with the public would cut out corruption. Instead, it increased unchecked brutality in certain neighborhoods. I saw it firsthand and I couldn't stand it. When I had the opportunity to leave the streets, I did. That's how I found my way here."

Captain Allen smiled and continued. "How long have you worked with Harriett?"

"Not long, I really just started as a reporter. For the last year I was learning the trade as an intern."

"Well, you're in good hands with Harriett. I love that woman. She's as loyal as they come. Did Harriett tell you how we came to know each other?"

"No."

"I guess she wouldn't. She keeps personal information to herself. About a year after my first wife died from that damn cancer, I met Angie and we eventually got married. I was surprised when she said yes. There aren't many women who'll decide to settle down with a man who has a kid. Ha, I think she fell in love with my little Emily before she fell in love with me."

"How does Harriett fit in?"

"I met Harriett through Angie. They're good friends. Without Harriett's help I could have lost Emily."

"What do you mean?"

"Pam was the name of my first wife. After she died

her family fought me for custody."

"But why would they want to take a daughter away from her father?"

"As you might imagine there's a load of hate in this world and Pam's family added to it. I could never understand how she survived growing up with them. When I married Angie they claimed I was raising my daughter in an unfit home."

"Because you remarried?"

"Because Angie is black. It didn't sit well with Pam's family."

"How did Harriett help?"

"Pam's family ran a huge hog farming operation in Missouri. And to show how small the world can be, Harriett's second cousin owned the adjacent property. Harriett got her cousin to sue the family for the hog stench. Funny thing, no one lived on her cousin's property. Hence, no one had to deal with the smell. All that didn't matter, Pam's family was set to lose a load of money in the suit."

"I smell more than hog stench. Maybe a bit of blackmail?"

"Blackmail is such strong word. In this case I prefer

persuasion. In the end Pam's family backed out of their custody fight, and in exchange Harriett's cousin signed a document stating he would never bring a suit against them for their stench. You got to love it. Their own rotten smell brought them down."

"My Grandmother has a saying, *se puede lavar la suciedad de la piel, pero no la de su alma.* It means you can wash the dirt off your skin but not from your soul."

"I like that. Now, enough about me. Harriett said you have a photograph to show me."

"Yes, here it is. It's of Ashworth. He's standing alongside other cops, his accomplices, who have all been arrested. This cop on the end though, I don't recognize him. I'm hoping you can get a name for me."

Captain Allen smirked. "That's Gary Bell. He was on the force for 19 years before we let him go."

"He was fired?"

"Yep, one too many domestic disputes. His wife Patricia finally filed charges against him for a beating he put her through. Gary was mad as a hornet when he found out he'd be missing a 20 year pension by a couple of months, but my hands were tied."

"Do you have an address for him?"

"I heard his wife took him back. Maybe you can find him at his last known address. Let me check the file."

"Thanks, this really helps."

Captain Allen picked up his phone and dialed an extension. In less than a minute a secretary walked in with Gary Bell's file.

"Ah, here's the address. The place isn't too far from here. Just up the way on Bunker Hill. What do you need from this guy? Are you thinking he was one of Ashworth's accomplices?"

"I never saw him with Ashworth, so I'm guessing he wasn't involved. But since he's in this photo he might know something about Ashworth that can help."

"Alejandra, this guy has a temper. I can go with you."

"I need to do this on my own. I don't want him spooked when I tell him Ashworth is dead, assuming he doesn't already know. Thanks for everything."

§§§§§§

The address for Gary Bell took me over the second

street tunnel to a weathered apartment building that sloped down a hillside. The only redeeming quality of the place appeared to be its full view of the downtown skyline. I made my way to an outside staircase and followed a corridor that wrapped around the side of the building to apartment #9. The door opened before I could even knock.

My presence surprised the disheveled middle-aged woman who stood in the doorway. "Whoa."

"Patricia?"

"Yeah."

"Sorry to bother you. I'm looking for Gary Bell."

"I got two things to say to you, Sister, that jackass doesn't live here and I'm on my way to work."

"Do you think you can spare a minute so I can ask you a couple of questions? I can walk with you."

The lanky woman brushed me to the side, slammed her front door closed, and locked it. She turned toward me and demanded, "Who's asking?"

"My name is Alejandra Marisol. I'm with the *Times*. I came to ask Gary about his friend, John Ashworth."

"John. He's another jackass. That's all I have to say."

The woman picked up her pace as she trotted down

the stairs. Following close behind I asked, "Do you know where I can find Gary?"

"Hell if I know."

I maneuvered in front of her. "I really need to speak with him."

"Look, I kicked him out close to a year ago. I don't know where he's living."

"Okay, thanks for your time. If you think of anything I can be reached at this number."

I gave her my card and started to walk away disappointed. Then Patricia yelled, "You can try the Olympic Auditorium. That's where he was working security when I kicked him out. If you see that SOB tell him he owes me money."

Chapter 6

MAN OF A THOUSAND MASKS

I opened the door to my unit when *Tía* Carmen called out. *"M'ija,* you're home. You've been gone all day. Come and sit with me."

Living in the same fourplex allowed for unplanned visits. Today, given what I had seen, I wanted to be alone and free to retreat into my shell before trying to find Gary Bell.

I pushed past my need for solitude. "Hey Carmen. I've been working to get some leads on those men who were found murdered in Belvedere Park."

"Horrible, *M'ija.* I can't believe this damn nightmare isn't over."

"The sight I saw, no one should witness. I have a lead though. I need to see if I can find this friend of Ashworth's. He may be working at the Olympic Auditorium."

"Really, M'ija? Are you going over there?"

"I'm going tonight. There will be wrestling at the Auditorium and I'm hoping he'll be there."

"Me and Jaime want to go with you."

"I'll be safe. I just want to talk with this guy."

"*M'ija*, I need to go. I need to think about something else. Okay, *M'ija*?" Carmen looked worried.

"What's going on?" I asked.

"I need to talk to you about something."

I sat close to Carmen on her glider. She grabbed my hands and spoke softly. "Jaime brought me to the doctor today. I didn't want to go, but he made me."

"Made you, why?"

"He noticed some blood oozing from my right breast."

"From where, a cut?"

"No *M'ija*, my nipple."

My heart sank with dread. "*Tía*, how long has this been going on?"

"Oh *M'ija*, I don't know. For a while I think, but I thought it would go away. I didn't want to think about it. I figured the blood was from a *pinche* pimple. After all, nothing ever came out of Te or Ta before, not even a drop of milk from me."

"Te or Ta?"

"I named them, *M'ija*. My left breast is Te and

my right one is Ta. Together that makes *Teta*, you know, Spanish for tit."

Carmen laughed and I couldn't help but do the same. "Oh, Carmen."

"The doctor, he checked me, said they need to do surgery, right away. He told me I'm going to lose a breast, my Ta."

"Does he think you have cancer?"

"Yes, *M'ija*."

Tears welled in the corners of my eyes. Cancer was in Carmen's body and she was dying. The heavy weight of longing started to pool and press into my chest. I didn't know what was worse, seeing someone die over time or in an instant, like my mom, with no warning. The sound of the car hitting her, the sight of the mangled body, my hands on her skin as I felt life slip away - the stinging memory of my mom's death wrapped its grip around my throat making it hard to breathe.

I saw Carmen's mouth move, but I couldn't hear a thing. "*M'ija*."

Carmen shook me hard and yelled. "*M'ija*, can you hear me?"

Like waking from a nightmare, I was back. Carmen knew where I went. "I miss her too, *M'ija*. I'm not going away, not anytime soon."

The pressure in my chest started to lighten. My heart no longer raced and I could breathe again. "I'm okay. I'm sorry, *Tía*."

"It's okay, *M'ija*. This is a shock for me too. But one good thing, Sumire came by earlier and took a mold of my breasts, for how they say it, posterity." Carmen rocked back and forth with a raucous laugh. "No one wants to see any part of their body torn away. I wasn't able to make a mold of my leg when I lost it to the sugar diabetes. Now with Sumire's help, I'll have a mold of my *tetas*." Carmen looked down at her breasts. "I guess I won't be needing a bra anymore, at least not a bra for two."

"When is the surgery?"

"In a couple of days. Jaime will take me."

"But you just met Jaime. I can take you."

"*M'ija*, don't be like that. I feel lots for Jaime already, and he feels the same way too. We nearly died together because of that *pinche* Ashworth. *M'ija*, he makes me feel good. I never had anybody ask me what I want, or what

I like. He wants to know how to please me. I didn't even know sex could be like this. All those years married to my husband, Mundo. He never cared about me. Jaime can touch this spot..."

It was too much for me. "Don't say it. You're my *tía*. I don't want to hear about you and Jaime."

"Okay. So we're going with you tonight, right? *Mil Máscaras* is wrestling."

"I'll take you to the Auditorium, but you guys will have to be on your own."

"No problem, *M'ija*. Maybe when you're done you'll have a little time to see *Mil Máscaras* do his stuff against Suni War Cloud, Goliath, or the Golden Greek. Oh that Golden Greek, I don't like his eyes. They spit fire *M'ija*, but *Mil* will snuff it out. I'd love to see *Mil* get the Golden Greek's head into a scissor lock, the one he can make with his legs. You've seen it, right?"

"Yeah, on TV."

Carmen snarled and grimaced as she threw her prosthetic and one good leg in the air and crossed them to show me how the Mexican wrestler would use his lower limbs to grip his opponents head into a vise grip.

"Oh *M'ija*, I'm excited. Cancer can wait. It's all about my 'Man of a Thousand Masks' tonight."

§§§§§§§

By the time I parked in the lot on 18th Street and Olympic Avenue, Carmen and Jaime had donned their own *Mil Máscaras* wrestling masks.

Jaime spoke with pride. "What do you think of mine, Alejandra?"

"I love that black and white spider image."

"I'm wearing the shark, *el tiburón*, *M'ija*. Like it?"

"You guys look great."

Jaime handed me a mask. "Don't think we forgot about you. Just in case you're able to join us for a couple of rounds. I call this one, *Señor Rayo*, for the lightning bolts on each side."

"Thanks, Jaime. I'll have the mask in my pocket just in case."

Carmen and Jaime left for the bouts and I cruised the perimeter of the auditorium in search of Gary Bell. After making a complete circle I couldn't find anyone with a short fireplug frame, long face, and prominent square jaw. I bought a ticket to try my luck inside.

As soon as a lanky Jimmy Lennon dressed in his trademark black tuxedo stood in the center of the ring to announce the next bout, pandemonium erupted. "Tonight, in the right corner we have former champion and member of the Canadian Wrecking Crew, the Goooooolden Greeeeeek."

Jimmy Lennon held onto letters and didn't let them go as he introduced the contenders. "In the left corner from Mexico we have the 'Man of a Thousand Masks,' you know him as *Miiiiiil Máscarassssss.*"

The crowd exploded. Men waved their fists in the air. Women clamored for a better view by stepping onto their seats and jumping with frenzy. Like Jaime and Carmen, many in the crowd wore traditional *Lucha Libre* masks in celebration of the free form style of wrestling that *Mil Máscaras* helped to make popular.

The two wrestlers shook hands and broke for their corners, but while *Mil Máscaras* had his back turned the Golden Greek clipped him from behind. The cheap shot brought *Mil Máscaras* to his knees. The crowd jeered and I caught myself screaming, "Boo." I wanted to keep watching but I needed to focus on finding Gary Bell.

The thick crowd made it clear I'd be hard pressed to find anyone. I tracked down a security guard. "I'm looking for Gary Bell."

"He's handling the tombs tonight."

"Tombs?"

"The locker rooms downstairs."

I nodded my appreciation. When I found the stairs I saw what had to be an older Gary Bell standing at the bottom. "Gary?"

"Yeah. Who are you?"

 "I worked for John Ashworth."

"Work? Right."

Gary took his time to look me up and down. "Let me guess, he's screwing you."

A "yes" response wouldn't be entirely wrong. Ashworth had screwed me, but I knew that's not what Gary Bell meant. Nevertheless, I was happy Gary spoke in the present tense; it meant he didn't know Ashworth was dead nor the circumstances involved. I kept pace with Gary's train of thought and confirmed his assessment. "You could say that."

"What do you want?"

"I have bad news. John's dead."

Gary kept a straight face. "Haven't seen John in a while. Wouldn't really know the difference, him dead or alive. How did you find me here anyway?"

"Your wife, Patricia."

"After all these years that woman still doesn't know when to keep her mouth shut. How did you find Patricia?"

I thought quickly. "John's address book."

"Since you're here, might as well give me the details. How? When did he die?"

"Two days ago. He took his own life."

Gary laughed. "You got to be kidding me. John committed suicide? Never saw that happening, not in a million years."

"Why do you say that?"

"John thought a lot of himself. At least the John I knew."

Gary paused, "I have to check the basement out."

"Can I follow you?"

"I guess."

"How did you meet John?"

"We shared a patrol car for a short time and then we met back up working Vice."

I pulled out the photograph of Ashworth with his buddies. "Do you remember this picture?"

"Those were different days. I'd only been on the force for about a year."

"Why did you lose contact with John?"

"Different interests. Look, why all the questions?"

"Trying to piece some stories together for a eulogy."

Gary was clearly agitated. "I don't have any stories."

I needed to try another angle. "That's too bad. Shirley will be disappointed."

"You talking about his ex-wife?"

I nodded.

"Wow, that woman had a hot ass on her. Too bad she had a mouth that wouldn't quit. Always nagging that one. So you're looking for stories? Any story I shared wouldn't be fit for a funeral. We weren't saints."

"What do you mean?"

"Let's just say when you work Vice opportunities to make extra cash pop up from time to time."

I saw an opening. "Is that because you came across

people in compromising positions?"

"Where did John find you anyway? He always did like 'em young."

"How young?"

"Too young for my taste. But you, you're not too young."

Gary Bell disgusted me but I needed him right now. "It sure would be nice to spend time with an old friend of John's."

"I should be done by midnight."

What was I doing? I didn't want to be alone with this guy. I had to try and get what I needed now. "Before we meet can I ask you one more question?"

"Sure."

"I found some other photos at John's. They were black and white Polaroids. In one of them a nude woman is tied to the bed with a man on top of her. Do you think the photo had something to do with finding people in compromising positions?"

"Can't help you."

Gary Bell's quick response and lack of expression told me he was holding back. I moved in closer. He could feel my breath on his cheek. "I understand if you don't want to talk about it."

Gary pulled back and fired at me. "You cheap whore. I'll wipe the floor with your ass. Get the hell out of here."

I hadn't expected the rage now spreading across Gary Bell's face. I turned and walked fast. He didn't let up. "I'll beat you for fun."

I couldn't create distance quick enough for my comfort. When I finally stopped I found myself in the middle of a hallway that opened onto a bank of unused locker rooms. In my desperation to get away from Gary Bell I made a wrong turn and got lost. Unlike the chaos upstairs, the basement was eerily quiet with no one in sight. As I turned to retrace my steps the lights went out. The darkness made it clear why they called this place the tombs; the porous concrete walls around me closed in and sealed me in like a leaden crypt.

I had to keep calm and not panic. I knew if I stayed my course I would eventually find the stairs. I reached into my pocket and applied a cool layer of lipstick. The oily film now coating my lips filled me with a sense of power and strength, and not too soon. A couple of steps into my stride I heard the sound of footsteps echo out of the blackness. I ran and the footsteps behind me kept pace. It had to be Bell on my ass. As I raced down the hall I could see light descending out of a stairwell. I quickly turned and climbed the two flights of stairs as fast as I could. When I reached the main floor I shot out of a tunnel and onto a narrow path lined with cheering wrestling fans on both sides. I threw on the *Lucha Libre* mask with lightning bolts, the one Jaime gave me, to blend with the crowd. The teeming hoard of people lining both sides of the path wouldn't let me break through. I could hear Bell on my heels making loud guttural sounds. I turned to see he had donned his own *Lucha Libre* mask with an image of a wolf. No one was helping me. Instead I heard the crowd start to mimic Bell's animal sounds, and then I realized I was on the contender's runway, making a beeline for the ring.

I reached the edge of the ring with no choice but to pull myself up using the ringside ropes to join the Golden Greek and *Mil Máscaras*. Johnny Lennon reached for his microphone and announced the Wolfman at which point the man chasing me entered the ring. The crowd went crazy. The auditorium seemed to levitate from the deafening cheers. It hadn't been Gary Bell chasing me at all.

Johnny Lennon shot a puzzled look my way. I could see Lennon's mind scramble as he improvised. "And joining the Wolfman tonight is his special guest, Canine Thunderrrrrrr."

I was in trouble now. I walked over to Johnny and tried to explain but it was too late. *Mil Máscaras* grabbed me from behind and with one hand lifted me up and spun me as if I were a clump of pizza dough. He then threw me into the air and caught me with his legs before I hit the ground. Unable to move I could see the Wolfman preparing to mount an attack as he bounced off the ropes and landed, full body, onto *Mil's* chest. The full weight of the Wolfman forced *Mil* to release his leg hold on me. That's when the Golden Greek pivoted and set his sights in my direction. As Carmen had described, the Greek's eyes spat fire. I needed to quickly get out of the ring. I put my gymnastics training to use. I threw my head back and let my body follow in one smooth move to catapult me into a series of back flips that brought me to the edge of the ropes. The crowd was relentless in their applause and I could hear them chant, "Thunder, Thunder, Thunder," but no matter how much they cheered they couldn't keep me in the ring. I grabbed the top rope and used it to fling away from the bout.

Carmen and Jaime were there to greet me ringside. "*M'ija*, what the hell is going on? Are you okay?"

"I thought Gary Bell had turned into the Wolfman."

"*M'ija*, did you get hit hard on the head? You're talking crazy stuff right now. No one can turn into a Wolfman *M'ija*, not without a full moon."

"No jokes right now. I'll explain later, just get me home.

"Of course *M'ija*, home it is."

Chapter 7

STRAIGHT SHOT ON THE ROCKS

I picked up the ringing phone. It was Harriett. "I happened to walk by when the receptionist took a message for you. A woman by the name of Patricia Bell phoned. She's hot. The receptionist tried to calm her, but no luck. This woman wants you to meet her tonight at her job, Lucky's Bar in Rampart, west of downtown. Alejandra, is there anything to worry about?"

"No, I'll take care of it."

§§§§§§§

At the corner of a lonely bank of houses off Beverly Boulevard sat Lucky's Bar. The blinking neon sign that read "Cold Beer" in the window was about the only thing that suggested life existed inside. Before I even stepped foot in the place the acrid smell of stale cigarettes and day old liquor jarred my nostrils. I took one deep breath and pushed through a black curtain that covered the entrance. I immediately spotted Patricia behind the bar serving a drink to an older man busy using matchbooks to build a structure of sorts. When I reached the counter, she motioned for me to take a seat at the end of the bar away from the other patrons. She wasted little time approaching me. The hot glare in her eye told me to be prepared for a tongue lashing, maybe more.

"You see this?" She pointed to the black eye she tried to hide with a caked layer of beige make-up concealer. She didn't let up. "This is your fault. I'm lucky he didn't kill me."

"I'm sorry. I never meant for anything to happen to you. I found him at the Olympic like you told me. I told him Ashworth was dead and asked him about a couple of photos I found. The man went crazy."

I could see Patricia's face relax. "So you got a taste of the bastard?"

"Sure did."

Like turning a switch Patricia's voice softened. "He's really more bark than bite."

"That black eye on your face says something different."

"It's the only thing he knows. His father and mother

used to beat him. I guess you could say he learned his ways from his parents."

"I don't think you asked me here to convince me Gary Bell is a great guy. Did you?"

"No, I didn't. The photo you described to him got him real scared. I know Gary well enough to know that when he's scared he turns into a crazy man. He can't control what he's feeling. I guess that's why I still love him."

"What did he say to you?"

"He couldn't believe John was dead. He told me John would never take his own life unless he had to."

"What do think he meant by that?"

"I asked if he thought John killed himself because he couldn't bear some sort of pain. He looked at me as if I were nuts. Told me I had it all wrong, that John had to kill himself or be killed. He said the photo you described was the reason, and that the father and the son would be coming after him now that John was dead."

"Who are the father and the son?"

"I asked him, but he didn't answer."

"What happened between the two of them? Why did John stop talking to Gary?"

"I don't know. They used to be close. When Gary worked with John he even spent all his free time with the man. Shit, I never saw my own husband. Then one day John shut him out. Gary never told me what happened. But secretly, I was happy they weren't friends anymore."

"How so?"

"There was something not right about John. I didn't like the fact that John took advantage of Gary's gambling habit to convince him to blackmail people. Gary told me when they'd bust a whorehouse sometimes they'd find important people they could pressure for money. Gary was always in need of cash." Patricia pointed to her black eye. "After Gary hit me he told me he regretted the blackmailing and the other stuff John got him mixed up in."

"What other stuff?"

"I don't know. He never talked about it."

"Patricia, do you know where I can find Gary? If he's in danger then maybe I can get him to go to the police."

"Gary? Go to the police? There's no way he'd ever do that. He's got too much pride. He blames LAPD for taking away his pension."

"Why doesn't he blame you? Didn't you report him

to LAPD Internal Affairs in the first place?"

"How do you know about that?"

"It was Internal Affairs who helped me find you."

"Huh, I don't expect you to understand. In the end Gary understood I did what I had to do, but that still didn't give LAPD the right to take away what he worked hard to earn."

"You're right, I don't understand. Regardless, do you know where I can find him? I think he may be in danger. Right now, I just want to help."

"I do still love him. I want him safe. Don't let him know you got this from me. He's staying at the Cecil Hotel, 6th and Main."

§§§§§§§

When I made the call to Captain Allen he agreed to meet me at the Cecil Hotel. I sure didn't want to be by myself when I talked to Gary again. When I arrived a sea of patrol cars and a coroner's van were parked outside. I had a gut feeling everyone was here for the man I needed to question.

"Alejandra."

I turned to find Captain Allen. "What's this all about?"

"Gary Bell is dead."

"No, no, no."

"A cleaning lady found Bell in the bathtub. The detective on the case is thinking suicide or accident."

I was emphatic. "Not possible."

"We'll have to leave that up to the medical examiner, although from a quick look at the scene I'd have to agree with you."

"Tell me more."

"I saw a hot pastrami sandwich in the room, warm to the touch and out of its wrapper. Not sure why a guy would buy a sandwich and get ready to eat it if he planned to take a bath."

"I knew it. I just left Patricia Bell. She told me Gary was scared. He knew someone would come after him."

"Why did he think that?"

"I found Gary working at the Olympic Auditorium. I told him about Ashworth committing suicide."

"Did you tell him why?"

"No. I didn't tell him he did it to avoid prison for running a sex trade operation. But I did ask him about some photographs and that's when he got real angry. I thought he'd kill me."

"What photos? Like the one you showed me?"

"No, others. I don't want to say more. I can't say more."

"Alejandra, I can't help you if you don't tell me what's going on."

"Look, I appreciate what you've done for me already, but..."

"But what? I owe Harriett everything. I told her I'd do all I can to help you."

Captain Allen could see the apprehension in my face. "You don't trust me. Why would you after what Ashworth put you through? Alejandra, I'm not John Ashworth."

I paused and relented. "Captain Allen, I broke into a house and found some photographs."

"Whose house? Start from the beginning."

"I followed Detective Carr, the one investigating the Belvedere Park murders. He drove to Ashworth's house to conduct a search and when he left I used an open bathroom window to get inside. I found three photographs, the one I showed you and these two."

I handed over the photographs to Captain Allen. "After talking with Gary Bell's wife, I'm almost certain Gary and John Ashworth were blackmailing the men in these photos. Patricia told me Bell and Ashworth were involved in extortion."

A look of shock panned over Captain Allen's face. "Who else has seen these?"

"Harriett. She told me the older man is Judge Thomas, and the younger man, we don't know. Gary's death has to be linked to these photos and the Belvedere Park murders. Otherwise, it's too much of a coincidence. I think someone knows I went to see Bell and I think he was murdered because he knew something."

"That may be, but it's not as if these photos can be used as evidence given how you got them."

"I know, but if it weren't for me the photos would still be hidden in Ashworth's house."

"I'll see what I can do on my end. I'll try and talk to the detective on Bell's case. But I'll tell you right now I won't get much. My colleagues don't like Internal Affairs, which means they'll be unwilling to answer my questions. They think I'm out to betray them and they are often right."

"Don't people want answers?"

"Homicide detectives like cases that get solved and then cleared from their desks. I should know. I was one."

"Don't they care about the victims?"

"Honestly, Alejandra, there are too many victims. Even the ones who get prioritized, detectives can't afford to feel anything. The only way to survive the depravity is to put up a wall. Otherwise, the horror consumes you. I'm not going to make excuses for detectives who should try harder, but even if we assume these photos are tied to Gary's death then what you have is a potential rabbit hole with no end in sight."

"You're wrong. I know where the hole ends."

"Where?"

"At the gates of Hell."

Chapter 8

CIPHER

"*M'ija*, are you home?"

"Coming, Carmen."

I walked in from my outdoor patio to see Carmen and Sumire both dressed in bright yellow dresses with sun hats to match.

"*M'ija*, Sumire and I are going shopping. Want to join us?"

"I don't have the right outfit."

"Aren't these dresses cute, *M'ija*? Sumire made them for us. We're like a couple of blooming daisies."

Carmen choked on her last word and started to cry.

"*Tía*, what is it?"

"Bad luck, Jaime asked me to marry him. I'm going to die right after I found a man who really loves me: all 202 pounds of me."

"Remember what you told me? You've got a lot of living to do. The doctors are going to remove the cancer. All of it. If anyone can survive this it's you, *Tía*."

"Oh *M'ija*, I hope you're right."

"I'm glad you have Jaime."

Carmen took a shallow breath. "I want you with me when my time is close. Dying can be cruel *M'ija*, especially when death makes you feel all the pain of this world before it takes you. It's not like when we're born. Birth has mercy on us. It keeps us from remembering how it feels to be pushed through a tiny narrow *chocha*. And you know I don't like small spaces. What's the word for it?"

"Claustrophobia."

"That's it. I have claustrophobia. I'm happy I don't remember my birth, but my mom didn't feel the same way. She reminded me all the time of the pain I put her through. Telling me my head was too big. That no woman should ever have to endure what she did. Some women shouldn't be mothers, especially when they can't replace pain with joy. Anyway, you coming with us?"

"Of course, I'll come. Can we stop to get something to eat?"

"Now you're speaking my language."

As we neared the neighboring shopping district the smell of roasted *elote* ignited a grumbling in my gut.

Without a pause we each paid twenty-five cents for a grilled ear of corn skewered on a stick and dripping with butter. I garnished my treat with lime and a sprinkling of chili powder before taking my first bite. A flood of warm, tangy sweetness filled my mouth and within a couple of minutes my cob was bare.

"Where are we off to now?"

"Well *M'ija*, Sumire needs candy and I need shoe laces."

Sumire added to the list. "I also need food for Gato. He likes that new cat food brand, the one with the giant roaring lion on the package. He's sold on the advertising."

"Sumire, he's a cat. He doesn't know what's on the package." I said.

"Gato knows more than you think."

I didn't know why I tried to disagree. Sumire's cat, Gato, could do remarkable things. In her own right, Sumire was amazing too. I didn't know if she had an innate gift or learned it growing up in a Japanese internment camp, but she could see things no one else could.

Our first stop was the candy store. Sumire's request today was ten bags of M&M's. The owner loved seeing

Sumire. "I love that you always pick my candy. You know these were named after me. M and M for Manaka Makaido. My favorite color is yellow like your dress and the sun."

Sumire responded. "Without sunlight there's no color and no beautiful world to see."

We left and headed to Joe's. The large green high-heeled shoe that jutted from the building's façade read, Epstein Shoe Repair. Inside my senses were overtaken by the sight and smell of all things leather. Beyond the cash register I could see Joe Epstein at his workbench. He finished hammering a heel onto a boot and lumbered toward us. "Good afternoon Ladies, Joe Epstein at your service. How have you all been? I haven't seen you in a while. Are your soles in need of salvation today?"

Carmen laughed and answered, "Just a pair of brown laces, Joe."

Joe reached above his back counter to pull down the package. "That'll be an even forty cents for the laces. No cost for the smile. That's free for you, Carmen."

Joe Epstein was one of the happiest people I had ever met and he had good reason. When I was a kid Joe told me the Nazis forced him to board a railroad freight car along with others from his Warsaw neighborhood. Somehow Joe got on the train without a Nazi guard checking his weathered wooden cobbler box, which had an awl and stretching pliers in a bottom compartment. As soon as the train pulled out of the yard Joe set to work with his tools to pry open the bars on the lone window inside the car. Joe freed himself along with ten others that day.

Carmen put exact change on the counter and that's when I noticed the sign behind the register. "Hey Joe, do you still use the Capitol phone exchange?"

"Of course I do, I like the ring of it. I enjoy saying Capitol for the letters CA instead of 22. Then I add the last five digits for my phone number. Why have letters on the dial face of a phone if you're not going to use them?"

"I agree. You've made me happy, Joe, more than you can know."

"Well, good, I like everyone to leave here happy."

On the way to the Birds of a Feather pet store Carmen couldn't hold back her curiosity. "*M'ija*, since when do you get so excited over a phone number?"

"It's not just the number, it's that he uses the exchange. One of the murder victims etched five numbers into his leather belt, and to do it he had to really stretch his bound hands to make sure those numbers followed the name, ED, imprinted on the belt."

"So *M'ija*, you think ED represents an exchange?"

"It's worth a shot. Maybe I'll get lucky. Dial a number and get a murderer."

Sumire couldn't contain her excitement. "Let's go now, straight home, and dial. No time to stop for cat food. Gato will understand."

Once home I picked up the receiver and dialed. Using the phone's dial face I saw that both letters, E and D, corresponded to the number three. I followed them with the five I got from the leather belt. After four rings a recorded voice came on the line, "You have reached a number that is no longer in service. Please check the number and dial again."

I followed the directions, but no luck, the recorded voice was all I got.

Chapter 9

CLEAR AS WATER

I was happy to see Olivia when I arrived at the morgue. "I'm glad you're here. Hope you have something that can give me traction with the case."

"Alejandra, I was just starting to tell Armand what I found. I was able to analyze the tooth and bone samples. Turns out all the men, except for the eldest victim, were born and spent much of the last ten years of their lives in the same place: the south-eastern part of Mexico; most likely the state of Chiapas."

"And the eldest victim?" I asked.

He was from the north-eastern part of the country; the state of Coahuila."

With excitement and confidence Armand announced, "Oh my, I think that explains the Leukonychia striata."

Armand walked over to the freezer, opened a drawer, and pulled out the tray with the eldest victim. He called us over. "See the fingernails on this man? He has white bands running across his nails. I didn't make much of it at first, but now knowing where he's from it's likely arsenic poisoning caused the striations."

"*Primo*, are you thinking what I'm thinking?"

"You got it. We're on the same page."

Impatiently I chimed in, "I want to be on the page with you."

Armand explained, "Our Uncle, *Tío* Enrique, was from a town in the north-eastern part of Coahuila called San Juan de Sabinas. Practically every man in that town, like our *tío*, worked at the coal mine. *Tío* Enrique told us horror stories about his work in that mine. Even though he left that town and moved to Los Angeles, the mine never let *Tío* go. The daily exposure to coal dust and the arsenic used to process the coal took him away from us too soon. This man must have been a coal miner. I'd bank on it, especially since this victim also showed the type of lung damage that comes from breathing toxic particulate matter day in and day out."

Even though I was no closer to knowing who the men were or why they were killed, Armand and Olivia had given me an important lead.

"This gives me something. Do you think you can take

a picture of each of these men for me?"

"Sure thing."

"Great, I'm going to need them for my trip to San Juan de Sabinas."

"Alejandra, how do you feel about me going with you? I have some time coming to me and I think I can help. I know someone in Sabinas we can talk to."

"I'd like that, Armand. I'd like it a lot."

"Perfect, and by the time we get back maybe Olivia will have some more results for us."

Olivia playfully cut in, "Is that how it's going to be? You both go off to have fun and leave Olivia to do the work."

"*Prima*, you know it's not like that, but it sure would be great to have the results from the blood samples ready when we get back."

Confused, I asked. "What blood samples?"

Olivia explained, "I'm trying out this new technique in the lab, I call it DNA, deoxyribonucleic acid, fingerprinting. Armand thought it might be worthwhile not only to analyze the victim's teeth and bone for their oxygen content, but also their DNA."

I had a million questions. "DNA, do you mean chromosomes?"

"Yes and no. In every human cell, except for sperm and egg cells, there are 46 chromosomes, and each chromosome is comprised of DNA. Most of the DNA that each of us possess is identical, but there's a small percentage of our DNA that is more variable and therefore more likely to be different between individuals who aren't related. I've been playing around with a way to look at particular chromosome regions that have been identified to contain highly variable DNA sequences."

"I see. The DNA variability is much like the impressions that can be made from our fingertips." I said.

"You got it, but I predict with DNA fingerprinting the possibilities will be unmatched. We aren't there yet, but within a few years we should be able to isolate and analyze DNA from a drop of blood left at a crime scene. My analysis will be limited but I should still be able to see if any of the victims are related."

"I'll be ready for anything you can offer, Olivia."

"Let's keep our fingers crossed. I'm off to the lab. I'll see you two later."

Much time hadn't passed but I hoped Armand had some news on Gary Bell. "Anything on the drowning case?"

"There's no way I can call this one with any certainty."

"How can that be?"

"Determining whether a drowning is an accident, suicide, or murder is nearly impossible. The initial blood work shows he had a lot of liquor in his system so he could have drowned accidentally. And..." Armand paused, "...he was dressed."

"What does that mean?" I asked.

"A murderer will usually go out of his way to make a drowning look like an accident by undressing his victim."

"So you're telling me Bell wasn't murdered."

"I just don't know. If he drowned while alive and conscious I'd expect to see defense wounds, but there are none. I tried to determine if someone rendered him unconscious and then placed him in a tub of water to make it look like an accidental drowning."

"And?"

"Around the nose and mouth I found some paleness that could have occurred because of pressure caused by someone smothering him. But the discoloration is so slight, I can't be certain."

"How do you rule out suicide? How do know if Bell

was dead or alive before his body hit the water?"

"Water in the lungs usually indicates the person was alive, conscious or unconscious, before he drowned. There's no water in Bell's lungs."

"So he was killed before being placed in the tub."

"Not so fast. In a small number of people we've seen death result from what's called dry drowning; water doesn't get into the lungs in those cases. It happens when the vocal cords spasm causing the throat to constrict, sealing off the airway. Bell died from a dry drowning that resulted in cardiac arrest. I can't tell if he was dead or alive before he went under water. The cause of death has to be classified as undetermined."

"Armand, what about his shoes?"

"What do you mean?"

"Are Gary Bell's shoes still here?"

"Yes."

"I remember thinking about them when I saw his body being removed from his room. I wondered how white scuff marks got on the heels of those beautifully polished shoes. I forgot all about them until now."

"Let's take a look."

Armand examined the shoes. "Looks like painted plaster."

"Had he been dragged to the tub his shoes could have scraped against the wall."

"Good point. I'll bring it up to the detective. Maybe he can find evidence in Bell's room to corroborate, but I wouldn't count on it. The detective seemed pretty determined to close the case."

"Damn it, doesn't anybody care?"

"Alejandra, I care."

"I know you do. I guess in the end it doesn't really matter how Gary Bell died. He's dead and he can't help us. Now we have to hope Sabinas gives us an open door to something more concrete."

Armand looked at me, affectionately. "Are you sure you're in the right line of work?"

"What are you talking about?"

"It seems like private detective is more up your alley."

"Hmm, Alex Marisol, Private Investigator. I like the sound of it."

"Why Alex and not Alejandra?"

"I'd get more business if people thought they were reaching out to a man."

"But the cat would be out of the bag once they saw you."

"Sure, but if they didn't like what they saw I'd still have a chance to work my charm before they turned away."

Armand leaned in. "The way you worked your charm on me?"

I inched closer. "Dr. Gomez, I think it was the other way around."

This time I turned my head into his neck and breathed in his smell of sweet and salted musk. I couldn't get enough. I wanted to bathe in him. I parted my lips and pulled his mouth toward mine. I felt us both surrender. There was no better taste.

Chapter 10

EL GUSANO

We wasted little time securing a rent-a-car after flying into Laredo, Texas. Armand drove while I navigated the map and charted our two-hour drive into Mexico across the Rio Grande River. Barring any complications, I figured we could make it to Sabinas and the home of Nacho Candelaria before nightfall. Armand's Aunt Trini, *Tío* Enrique's surviving wife, arranged for us to meet Nacho, a tender and good soul as she had described. From the little I knew Nacho spent years working alongside *Tío* Enrique in the mines. He had even risked his own life to dig Enrique out of a pile of rubble after high levels of methane gas created an explosion, which killed twelve of their friends. Trini told us Nacho still knew a lot of men, *los mineros*, who worked the mine. I hoped Nacho could help by knowing some or all of the men found murdered in the truck bed.

By the time we arrived our Ford Pinto no longer looked white. The dust we stirred driving the unpaved roads left an uninterrupted brown film over the car's entire frame.

Hearing our car, Nacho emerged from his house to greet us.

"*Bienvenidos*. Welcome, Armand and Alejandra. I'm so happy, *muy feliz*. I hope it's okay for me to speak English while you are here, I don't get much chance since my father died."

I asked, "You grew up speaking English?"

"Yes, my father was from *Tejas*. Even though we lived here he wanted me to know English."

Nacho's voice was warm and inviting. I immediately wanted to know all about him. "When did your father move here from Texas?"

"Alejandra, it's dangerous to ask an old man about the past. History is my friend and I'm not stingy when it comes to words. It could be a long night."

"We have nowhere to go until tomorrow."

"Good. Come inside, I'll pour you a drink and fill your ears."

We followed Nacho inside and took seats at a weathered wooden table.

"I hope you like mezcal." Nacho placed a filled shot glass in front of each of us. "Food will be ready soon, I made *mole*. It's the one thing I can cook that tastes good. My wife, *mi amor* Imelda, she did most of the cooking, but she passed last year."

Armand responded, "Aunt Trini told me about Imelda. I'm sorry. We didn't expect you to make us dinner, but it sure smells good. Thank you."

"You're the nephew of my good friend, Enrique. I would have given my life for him. *Comida* and mezcal are nothing. Drink up."

As I let the agave derived spirit pickle my throat I realized I hadn't spent enough time acquiring a taste for the stuff. Nacho quickly refilled my glass and I realized there'd be no casual introduction; I would be spending intimate time with tequila's cousin.

My questions about the murdered men would have to wait. In keeping with his warning Nacho immediately immersed us in family history. "This is a picture of my father as a young boy. He's standing with my grandfather, my namesake, Ignacio Candelaria. The picture was taken in 1852, just before they stole my grandfather's *rancho*."

I pressed, "How does someone steal a ranch?"

"Manifest Destiny."

Armand asked for clarification. "Are you referring to

the United States' aggressive land grab?"

"You know about it. It was disguised as The Treaty of Guadalupe Hidalgo, signed to end the Mexican-American War. What a crime! That treaty created a new border for Texas along the Rio Grande and it called for Mexico to give up California, Arizona, New Mexico, and parts of Colorado, Nevada and Utah in exchange for little money."

Armand added to the history lesson. "Aunt Trini's family, as far back as they could remember, lived in California. They were *Californios*, native Californians. They eventually lost their land because of that treaty."

"So you know firsthand how greed works. For my grandfather, one thief by the name of Samuel Buchanan changed his fate. Even though the treaty recognized Spanish and Mexican land grants, Buchanan knew Mexicans like my grandfather had no political power to hold on to property after it became part of the United States."

Nacho took a sip of mezcal, "Samuel Buchanan used all his means to get what he wanted. Late one night he went to my grandfather's ranch with a group of men who were former Texas Rangers. They grabbed my grandfather and grandmother out of bed and dragged them outside. They forced my father, a young boy, to watch as they whipped my grandfather and raped my grandmother. They threatened to return the next night unless my grandfather signed over his property." Nacho stared at the photo of his father and grandfather. "Humans are like parasites. They are incapable of surviving without taking over a host."

"Do you know what became of Buchanan?" I asked.

"He followed in his father's footsteps and became a very rich man."

I followed with another question. "Who was his father?"

"A former slave trader from Missouri by the name of James Buchanan. He made his money trading African slaves with the likes of James Bowie and Jean Lafitte."

"Jean Lafitte the pirate?" Armand asked.

I was dumbfounded. "How do you know all of this?"

"I needed to understand the history that led to the loss of my grandfather's land. The more I learned, the more I realized Samuel Buchanan's greed descended from his father. You've heard the saying the fruit doesn't fall far from the tree?"

"Yes." Armand and I answered in unison.

"In the case of James and Samuel, they were part of the same fruit: Samuel the seed and James the flesh surrounding him. When eight-year-old Samuel Buchanan learned his father had died defending the Alamo he filled his heart with hatred and disgust for Mexicans. Samuel didn't care that Mexican *Tejanos*, who had called *Tejas* their home for generations, had also been killed fighting the Mexican army for independence. When the United States declared war on Mexico in 1846 Samuel Buchanan was one of the first in line to draw Mexican blood. He was ruthless. As a Texas Ranger he raided Mexican villages, set homes ablaze, raped women, hanged innocent civilian men, and shot children all in the name of securing a U.S. victory. Buchanan and his Ranger compatriots became notorious for their brutality. They lived up to the name the Mexicans had given them, *Los Diablos Tejanos* or Texas Devils."

"Nacho, have you ever taught history?" I asked.

"This house is my classroom."

I wanted more. "What happened to your grandparents after losing their land?"

"They came here and started again from nothing. Times were hard. All they had was agave. They ate the flowers, the stalks, and the sap. Catching and cooking up rodents was a treat for them. Things began to turn around when the coal mine opened. By that time my father was old enough to work and his wages helped put better food on the table and build this house. I don't remember a single day when my father didn't have a layer of black coal dust on his face and hands. My father wanted a different life for me. He didn't want me in the mines. He thought an education would protect me from the evil men in this world. But as I've learned, the only thing that protects you from the devil is being lucky enough not to cross his path. Evil is everywhere. Coming back home after my studies was just as good as any other place. Plus, Imelda was here and she didn't want to leave. She was *mi amor y mi vida*, my love and my life, from the day we met. I never regretted my decision to return and work the mines. I knew I could leave any time with the power of my mind. Books became my way of visiting the world outside of this town. I read about everything imaginable through Faulkner, Woolf, Calvino, Rilke, Neruda, Cervantes, I can go on and on. Words allowed me to transcend these walls, *como el gusano*."

Nacho had lost me. "Like the worm?"

"Yes, like the worm in this mezcal."

Nacho emptied the last bit of mezcal into my glass along with the worm that had settled at the bottom of the bottle.

"The worm in your glass is actually a larva preserved in one stage of its life. No longer capable of metamorphosis on its own. But once inside you, like the words on the page of a book, the larva will undergo a transformation, sprouting wings and taking flight. You'll have no choice but to get carried along."

Nacho's stories had held me captive and I had been their willing prisoner. I had expected to arrive, ask him a few questions, and leave.

"I think the *mole* is ready. Let me serve your plates."

Nacho returned from the kitchen with plates of chicken submerged in a smooth, dark brown sauce. The delicious aroma rose off my plate and I didn't hesitate to slice away a succulent piece of the breast meat for my first bite. The heat from the chili in the sauce rolled across the roof of my mouth and opened my senses to the taste of cocoa, cinnamon, peanuts, and garlic. My taste buds danced with delight.

"Please, you both traveled too far to hear me ramble on. How can this old man help you with your investigation?"

"Armand brought some photos for you to see. They're of five murdered men we believe are from this town."

Armand passed the photos to Nacho who proceeded to slowly shuffle through them.

"Do you recognize any of the men?" Armand asked.

"I know this man very well."

Nacho pointed to the photo of the eldest victim. "That's Eduardo Cuevas. He had a big mouth, that one. He always talked about leaving this place and making lots of money in the North. Then one day he told he met *el comedor del pescado grande*: his ticket to fortune."

Confused I asked. "The big fish eater?"

"I never knew what he meant. He always talked in riddles. It was his way of saying something that meant nothing, so I paid no mind."

"Where did he meet *el comedor*?"

"Eduardo said he met him in Los Angeles when he was visiting a friend. I always assumed that's where he moved. He left about two years ago and took several young miners with him."

Nacho pointed to the other photos. "These are the men who went with him. He promised them a rich life."

"Do you know their names?" I asked.

"No, they were real but invisible."

"What do you mean?"

"They all arrived together from the South not able to speak a word of Spanish. They were Native Mexican Indians. They may as well have been vermin the way everyone treated them. I tried to get to know them, but it was too late. Like the spider using its web to snare prey, Eduardo Cuevas used his limited knowledge of their language to take advantage of them. He manipulated them so they would trust him and only him."

"Did any family travel with them from the South?"

"No, they arrived from Chiapas alone."

I turned to Armand. "Did you hear that? Nacho just corroborated Olivia's test results. The younger men did grow up in Chiapas."

Armand challenged me, "Sure, but what good does it do us? We have no lead to follow."

"Yes, we do. We know Eduardo Cuevas took the men to Los Angeles. We just have to find out why."

"Would there be anybody who could tell us more about these men, Nacho?" I asked.

"Not anyone from here. They worked all day and then went home with Eduardo. If you could find the man they all left with, that might help."

"They left with another man from here?"

"He wasn't from here. He came, packed everyone into a van, and left the same day."

"What did he look like?"

"He was a white man. I remember his head was long for his body."

I pulled out the group picture with Ashworth and Gary Bell. "Do you see the man in this photo?"

"When I saw him he was much older, but it's the man on the end." Nacho pointed to Gary Bell.

"That's helpful. One more thing, all of the victims had one of their arms ripped off. Do you have any idea why someone would do that?"

Nacho rolled up his sleeve. On the inner part of his forearm there was a small tattoo. It showed a crisscrossed pick and shovel with the word Sabinas written at the top. "Most of us miners, including Eduardo Cuevas, had one of these. Maybe the killer knew it would tie him to Sabinas."

"Did the younger men have the same tattoo?" I asked with urgency.

"I doubt it. We get this tattoo as a symbol of honor, for giving our life over to the earth. Those other men weren't here long enough to earn the right, but who knows what Eduardo had them do. They were like innocent lambs doing whatever the wolf told them, for fear of being eaten."

"This is the second time a tattoo may hold an important key in this case."

Nacho questioned, "When was the first?"

"An earlier victim, a man by the name of Sergio Guerra, had a tattoo of a *calavera* on his tongue. That tattoo ultimately led us to Sergio's friends and then put us on path with a cold-blooded killer, Detective John Ashworth."

"A policeman?"

"Yes, and even though Ashworth is dead the killing hasn't ended. Someone is still out there."

"That means you'll need to have a little more mezcal. I have a special bottle. One with an extra large *gusano* for luck."

"Of course Nacho, but only if you tell us more stories."

"I can do more than that."

Nacho reached for his accordion and slipped it on. He set to work on his keys while expanding and compressing the bellows to create high-pitched harmonized vibrations.

"This is one of my favorites, a *Cumbia*."

The fiery tune brought Armand to his feet. He reached for my arm. "Time to dance the *Cumbia*, Alejandra."

I stood and melted into Armand's body. He wrapped his right arm tight around my waist and led me with his left hand across the living room floor as Nacho sang.

> *"La cumbia pa' que bailen con ganas*
> *La cumbia pa' que bailen con ganas"*

There was no doubt I lived the words Nacho was singing; dancing the *Cumbia* with desire. It would be just a matter of time before Armand and I would have to excuse ourselves so our bodies could engage in a different dance, a more intimate one.

Chapter 11

BEYOND FACE VALUE

When we arrived back in Los Angeles, I realized Armand was right. Even though Nacho identified Gary Bell and Eduardo Cuevas from photos, I had no lead to follow since both men were dead. I had nowhere to turn except for a visit to Detective Carr.

My attempts to speak with Carr on the phone got me nowhere. The detective made it clear he wanted nothing to do with me, but I wouldn't take no for an answer. Determined to talk with him, I drove to the Sheriff's Homicide Bureau and sat parked in my car. At 5:30 am, Carr arrived. I approached quickly, cutting off his path to the front door.

"Detective, can I talk to you?"

Carr didn't waste words. "I'm busy."

"I know, but if you could spare a minute. Please."

"One minute." Carr lifted his arm and stared at his wristwatch.

"Really, Detective."

"You said one minute, tick tock, tick tock."

I spoke quickly. "I came from a small town in Mexico, Sabinas-Hidalgo. It looks like the murdered men worked the mines in that town. The older victim, his name, was Eduardo Cuevas. He brought the younger men to the U.S. with the help of Gary Bell, a friend of Ashworth's and former LAPD detective."

"Your time is up. This case is closed."

"What do you mean?"

"What you've just said makes the case against Ashworth even stronger. Ashworth's friend brought the men here from Mexico and Ashworth killed them. The victims' time of death doesn't rule Ashworth out as a prime suspect. He could have committed the murders well before he took his own life. Plus, Ashworth's prints were found all over that truck. We have our man. The case is closed."

"Even if Ashworth did do it, you don't have the whole story."

"The LAPD accomplices we have in custody corroborate Ashworth's role."

"What accomplices? Did you speak with Detective Nadel?"

"Yes, we did. He told us Ashworth was responsible for all of it."

"Did you search Nadel's house?"

"Of course we did. We found nothing. I'm not wasting any more time with you."

As Carr started to walk away, I moved in front of him. "Don't you care? Detective Nadel must know something. He helped to run the sex ring with Ashworth."

"If you don't get out of my way you'll find yourself in a jail cell."

I moved to the side and Carr moved ahead. He turned back once to glare in my direction before entering the Bureau's doors.

§§§§§§

Carr was closing the case and I knew there was still someone out there, somebody other than Ashworth who was pulling the strings and calling the shots behind the scenes. My mind felt hazy and confused. I needed to collect my thoughts and I needed to eat. Even though the sun hadn't crested over the horizon I knew The Pantry would be open for business. I headed to 9ᵗʰ Street and Figueroa. It took less than ten minutes to clear my plate of skillet fried potatoes, two sunny side-up eggs, and a thick slice of grilled sourdough toast. The waiter commended me on my hearty appetite and tallied my bill. I saw him write the total, $1.85.

The waiter sparked my attention. "Would you mind writing the total again, but slower?"

"I'm not even gonna ask why. Here you go."

The waiter rewrote the total and I saw it again. "Wow."

"Wow, what?"

"I've never seen anyone write the number eight like you do. You write the number three and then loop it from the bottom to connect it to a backward number three."

"Never thought about it. Done it that way my whole life."

"Thank you, thank you so much." I plucked down a full dollar tip.

"I'll write the number eight all day for you for this kind of money. Thank ya, Miss."

I walked out of the restaurant and located a telephone booth. I dropped a dime and dialed. As I did before I used the two letters found on Eduardo Cuevas' belt, ED, as part of the Edison exchange. I followed the exchange with the five numbers scratched into leather belt, but this time using an eight instead of a three for the last number. After four rings a woman answered, "Saint Basil's Rectory." I didn't know what to say so I hung up the phone.

I had heard of St. Basil's. A lavish church fit for its upscale neighborhood; that's how I remembered it described. I needed to know why Eduardo Cuevas would use his last moments on Earth to leave a number to St. Basil's. The first order of business was to find out who ran the place.

Chapter 12

A MAN OF ONE ROBE

As expected, Harriett was seated in her office. What I didn't anticipate was to find Rocky at her side. I also didn't expect to see the dramatic effect of their new love affair on Rocky's appearance. Aside from the steel grey hair no one would guess he was 70; he looked much younger and more fit than usual.

Harriett called to me as I approached. "Alejandra, come on in. Rocky stopped by to take me to breakfast. Didn't you, Rocky?"

"We were just getting ready to leave. Harriett knows this great place at Grand Central Market."

I was firm. "Your breakfast will have to wait."

I threw an *LA Times* article with a picture of Monsignor Crowe onto Harriett's desk. "Anything strike you?"

Confused Harriett answered, "What should I be seeing?"

"Does Monsignor Crowe remind you of anyone?"

"Like whom, can you help me out?"

I reached into my pocket and pulled out the Polaroid photo with the woman tied to the bed. "Like the naked man in this picture."

Harriett studied the image. "Hmmm, maybe it's the same man, but I can't be 100 percent certain. The man in this Polaroid has to be at least 20 years younger."

"What do you know about Monsignor Crowe?"

"I know he's the backbone of the Archdiocese, as far as money matters and real estate holdings are concerned. Crowe has a reputation for being a financial wizard and he's Cardinal McCrudden's right-hand man."

"Well, I think Crowe is somehow involved in the Belvedere Park murders."

"That's unbelievable. What kind of information do you have?"

"One of the victims scratched five numbers into his leather belt. He did it in a way that the numbers followed his name, ED, which had been stamped into the belt. When I used ED as an exchange and dialed the number I reached Saint Basil's rectory. I did a bit of research and found out Monsignor Crowe is the pastor of Saint Basil's. I found this photo of him in the *Times* archive room."

Harriett was shocked. "Oh my, this is going to catch fire if what you're saying pans out."

"There's more. Turns out the murdered men worked the mines in a Mexican town, Sabinas-Hidalgo. I met a man there who knew the men. He told me the eldest victim, Eduardo Cuevas, moved to Los Angeles to find his fortune. A person Eduardo referred to as *el comedor del pescado grande*, planned to help him make his money."

"Alejandra, you'll need to translate."

"The big fish eater."

Impatient, Harriett pushed. "More translation, please."

"What do Catholics eat every Friday?" I asked.

Harriett's mouth parted wide as she stared at me incredulously, "The Monsignor is the big fish eater?"

"That's what I'm betting on, especially since Eduardo scratched the Monsignor's number into his belt. What can you tell me about Crowe's boss, Cardinal McCrudden?"

"He's a political master."

Rocky added, "He sure is. Harriett, tell her how he bamboozled the public, ripped us off."

"Ever hear about Proposition 3, Alejandra?"

"No."

"Not surprising, you were a baby, just two or three years old. It was a 1952 referendum that went on the ballot after the Governor signed legislation to end taxation of Catholic school buildings. A taxpayer's group spearheaded the referendum in a move to reverse the legislation. McCrudden was a huge fan of the Governor's legislation. After all he'd been hard at work consolidating Catholic influence in Southern California by increasing property holdings for the Archdiocese, and he didn't want to be on the hook for paying taxes on his real estate."

Rocky cut in, "Less taxes for him meant less money for the public."

"Rocky's right. The proposition failed, saving the Archdiocese a lot of revenue. It left the City of Los Angeles and the Los Angeles Unified School District without the funding it needed to support public schools, street maintenance, you name it."

Rocky cut in again. "The Cardinal got his way."

Harriett countered, "Not right away. With support from public school advocates the tax-exempt issue went before the voters again in 1958 as Proposition 16. In the run-up to the election the Cardinal used his clout to influence politicians and citizens alike. His investment paid off. He won by a two to one margin, thereby securing tax-exempt status for his Catholic schools."

I knew the answer but asked anyway. "Does he have politicians in his pocket?"

Emphatic, Harriett answered. "Yes. Look at what happened with Chávez Ravine."

"I remember my mom talking about a friend who lost her home in Chávez Ravine. The Cardinal was involved?"

"At least indirectly, and I'm sure it secured his role as a power broker in this city for a long time to come."

Harriett had my full attention. "Go on."

"In the early '50s the Cardinal represented a voice for Catholic traditionalists. His vocal anti-communist views were no secret. He saw Soviet and Chinese influence across the globe and at home in the United States as a growing threat to Christian ideals. He even utilized the Archdiocese newspaper, *The Tidings*, to warn parishioners of the communist threat and encourage them to participate in conservative activism."

Harriett had lost me. "But how is this related to Chávez Ravine?"

"In 1951, the Los Angeles Housing Authority began acquiring land from Chávez Ravine residents, most Mexican-Americans, by forcing them to accept meager cash payments for their property to make way for Elysian Park Heights. Elysian Park Heights was a proposed housing development that would include schools and playgrounds. For residents who refused to sell, the City used the power of eminent domain to forcefully evict them. All of this was happening while the Cardinal did all he could to make sure Elysian Park Heights was never built. He regularly denounced public housing as an example of socialism. He even tied the Elysian Park Heights project to a communist plot bent on taking control of Los Angeles. The Cardinal's views held considerable sway over people who bought into anti-communist fear mongering."

Harriet paused and with a look of disgust continued. "The fate of Chávez Ravine was sealed in 1953 when Norris Poulson was elected Mayor of Los Angeles. Like the Cardinal, Poulson used the fear of communism to win the election. He campaigned on a platform promising to end the construction of any new public housing including Elysian Park Heights."

"Harriett, Dodger Stadium now stands in Chávez Ravine. Did the Cardinal play a role in that land deal?"

"You mean with the Dodger's owner, Walter O'Malley? No evidence of that, but it sure is an interesting question. I've always wondered what the outcome would have been for Chávez Ravine and its residents if the Cardinal hadn't gotten involved. But he did, and now the bucolic hillsides of Chávez Ravine are gone. There's no housing development and Walter O'Malley makes millions off his stadium. It all feels eerily unsettling when you consider that McCrudden turned down a profitable job on Wall Street to enter the priesthood. He wasted no time making his ecclesiastical ascension to become Archbishop and then Cardinal. He's created an Archdiocese more akin to a wealthy conglomerate. If he hadn't joined the priesthood I'm convinced he would have become a Wall Street magnate."

Rocky quipped. "Anti-communist fear mongering, the 'Red Scare;' it's like the circus clown."

Confused, I asked. "What do you mean?"

"The circus clown keeps the lion from eating the ringmaster. The Cardinal and Poulson used a circus clown to keep the public from eating them."

"Rocky, who's the circus clown?"

"Propaganda, Sweety. It's dirty propaganda."

"What you both are telling me might jive with what I've been thinking. Remember this photo?"

I pulled out the picture of Ashworth standing alongside fellow LAPD officers. I pointed to the man on the end. "Captain Allen identified this man. His name is Gary Bell and he was found dead a while ago. I'm betting he was murdered. I met with his estranged wife and she verified what you thought. She told me her husband and Ashworth were involved in blackmailing schemes. Harriett, if we assume Monsignor Crowe is the man in this photo then it's possible Ashworth and Bell were blackmailing him. And then comes the next question, did McCrudden know about it?"

Harriett shook her head. "Questions that need answers."

I added, "There's more. My contact in Mexico told me Gary Bell brought Eduardo Cuevas and the other Belvedere

Park murder victims to Los Angeles. The pieces are here, but I don't know how they fit together."

Rocky interjected, "Well Ladies, I know someone who might be able to help. My friend, William Dubin, is a former priest who had run-ins with McCrudden. They didn't like each other, and if I remember right he told me their troubles started around Chávez Ravine. He may be able to give you info on McCrudden and if nothing else tell you if the man in the Polaroid is Crowe or not."

I questioned, "How did you meet a former priest?"

"I met William after my friend Viola was murdered."

"Viola?" I asked.

"Viola Liuzzo. She was killed right around the time your mom died. I didn't know her long. We met in 1965 during a demonstration in Alabama working with our black friends to win everyone's right to vote."

Harriett stroked Rocky's arm. "I remember the time as if it were yesterday. I'm sorry about Viola."

"Thanks, Sweetness."

"How was Viola killed, Rocky?" I asked.

The Klan killed her and that bastard J. Edgar Hoover ran her name through the mud. Made her out to be a communist, drug addict, and a whore to conceal the fact that an FBI informant was with the Klan when they murdered her." Rocky shook his head. "Last time I saw her we were enjoying cold iced tea in Selma, Alabama on the porch of Mrs. Adela Jefferson. Adela had stories to make you laugh and others to make you cry. On one visit she told Viola and I how she used to help run a medical clinic where a woman could go to have an abortion. She coined a phrase, *None but the Father*. I asked her what it meant and Great Caesar's Ghost, I couldn't believe the answer."

Rocky had my full attention. "What did the phrase mean?"

"Those nuns got pregnant, and it happened after they were raped by a priest, a father, from the local parish. And those nuns couldn't do a damn thing about it. So they took care of things the only way they felt they could."

"Rocky, that's horrible."

"Sure as hell is. That's why I say, just because a man wears the cloth it don't mean a damn thing. There are many good priests, but you're bound to get a rotten apple in the bunch every now and again, just like McCrudden. You know, William Dubin was one of the priests who wanted to pay respect to Viola's memory by having a special mass for her. And for that, McCrudden suspended him from the priesthood."

"I'm anxious to meet your friend."

"Let me give him a call and see if we can pay him a visit tomorrow."

"Perfect."

Chapter 13

NEWS FROM THE MOUNTAIN TOP

On our way to see William Dubin, Rocky told me the former priest had married. I wondered aloud. "Do you think the Church will ever allow priests to marry?"

Rocky laughed, "No possible way. Although I will say, the chance of priests marrying is greater than women gaining entry into the priesthood. The Church is really missing out. Take me for example, I might find myself going to church on a regular basis if I could get on my knees and confess my sins to a woman. Absolution would feel so good."

"You're too much."

"I'm only speaking the truth."

When we reached William Dubin's ranch style home, rows of colored flowers stretched across the front yard. A slight man with a full beard dropped his pruning shears and approached as Rocky's Lincoln came to a stop.

"My dear friend, Rocky, you've arrived at the perfect time of year. The alstromeria, gerbera, and daffodils couldn't be in better display."

"William, it's all quite lovely."

"Flowers, there's not a single bad thing about them. Pure beauty, unlike the man you came here to ask me about."

"William, this is Alejandra, my adopted daughter."

"Pleased to meet you. Rocky filled me in a little. How may I help?"

I dove right in, "Do you recognize the man in this photo?"

I passed the Polaroid to William. He took his time looking at it. "Am I supposed to know him?"

"I was hoping you'd tell me it's Monsignor Crowe."

"I can see a likeness, but I'm not certain. This picture doesn't give me a full frontal view of his face. If it's the Monsignor, he's much younger here."

"What can you tell me about Crowe?"

"He's the Cardinal's finance wizard. He runs the Archdiocese. I didn't have a real association with him other than attending some of the same public services and events."

"If this is Crowe then it's likely he and his boss, Cardinal McCrudden, are involved in a case I'm working on. I don't know how you can help, but we thought if you could tell us more about McCrudden it might shed some light."

"Ah, a fishing expedition. Well, let's see if I can give you something a bit bigger than a morsel of bait on the line."

"Rocky told me the Cardinal pretty much fired you from the priesthood."

"That's about right. The Cardinal grew tired of me. I had been a thorn in his side for some time, and it started with Chávez Ravine. I had been a priest in Chávez Ravine, at *El Santo Niño*. I loved that chapel. When the city decided they were going to tear down people's homes and build a housing project it was devastating, but we held out hope that the new residences would be good for the people in the long run. We had no other choice than to feel optimistic, but that didn't take away the heartbreak of seeing people cheated out of their homes. More tragedy came when the housing project never got built. The Cardinal used his influence to make sure of it."

I pressed, "Did you try to fight him on the housing project?"

"I sure did, but I couldn't match his power. But my battles with the Cardinal didn't begin and end there. Things worsened between us when I learned Walter O'Malley needed one last parcel to secure all the land he needed for his new stadium. Did you know the plot of land where my little church, *El Santo Niño*, used to stand is where the centerfielder, Willie Davis, now catches those high fly balls in Dodger Stadium?"

"I had no idea."

"My heart and *El Santo Niño* were one. When I found out O'Malley needed the *El Santo Niño* land I contacted the Cardinal and pleaded with him not to sell. The Cardinal told me that the Archdiocese no longer owned the land. When I asked him to tell me who did, he said I had no business concerning myself with the fiscal matters of the diocese. At that point I had no other choice but to find out who did own the land. Have you heard of Clay Whitman?"

"No."

"Clay Whitman happens to be one of the biggest developers in Los Angeles. I found that out in 1952 when the Cardinal transferred the title of the *El Santo Niño* land to a holding company that Whitman owned, the Gateway Real Estate Limited Liability Company. From all accounts the Archdiocese didn't receive any money in the deal which seemed strange."

Rocky questioned, "You say 1952, that would be

before Walter O'Malley thought about bringing the Dodgers to Los Angeles?"

William was quick to respond. "Corruption is like devil grass. Its invasive deep roots take hold and strangle everything good around it. I believe the housing project was a front. Sure there may have been a few folks with good intentions who truly thought new housing would be built, but the power brokers, the devil grass, knew all along they would prevail and the Dodgers would leave Brooklyn for Los Angeles."

William couldn't give me answers fast enough. "Okay, but why would McCrudden give Whitman the land for free?"

"I questioned the Cardinal about it, but of course he didn't have an answer. What I did get was the loss of my parish and a reassignment as a hospital chaplain. I had no choice but to drop the issue."

I pressed again. "Do you think McCrudden took part in the backroom deals to get the Dodgers here?"

"Of course I do. The *El Santo Niño* deal proved it to me. Plus, the Cardinal's stance on the proposed new stadium was no secret."

Rocky piped in, "No secret is right, the Cardinal even went on television to endorse the Dodger Stadium ballot referendum."

William concurred, "That's right."

William's story introduced detours I hadn't expected. "I wonder if McCrudden's been involved in ongoing deals with Clay Whitman."

William spoke his thoughts. "It would not surprise me. If I were you, I'd follow the money."

I had one more thing on my mind. "A man by the name of Gary Bell was found dead. I think he was murdered. Before his body was discovered Bell's wife told me he was worried the father and the son would be coming after him. William, are Cardinal McCrudden and Monsignor Crowe ever referred to as the father and son?"

"No. The Father and Son are designations reserved for the Holy Trinity. Together with the Holy Spirit they describe three divine persons in one God. Alejandra, maybe Gary Bell was using a metaphor."

As we made our way back home we passed perfect rows of orange trees, followed by lemon, and then grapefruit. I started to think about how fields are plowed, seeds are sown, fruit is grown, picked, and eaten. If only life were managed like an orchard with clearly defined paths. But life is never a clearly defined path. Five dead bodies in the back of a pickup truck, a cardinal with interests beyond the church, a real estate developer with ties to the Archdiocese, a possible metaphor with no known meaning, all proof that nothing was clear.

Chapter 14

DIRTY MONEY

William Dubin's words, "follow the money," played over and over in my head. For the Los Angeles Archdiocese following the money translated into property. I had no better place to start than the County Clerk's Office where I could request a record for all Archdiocese real estate holdings.

Harriett worked fast to have another one of her contacts ready to help me when I arrived at the Clerk's Office. In quick order Harriett's friend, Shirley, handed me strips of microfilm with the property title data I needed. I scrolled up and down a long list of properties before focusing my attention on the *El Santo Niño* Chapel address. I wanted to verify that McCrudden had indeed turned over the chapel property to Clay Whitman's holding company as William Dubin claimed. When I found the address I saw that, in 1952, a transfer of title from the Roman Catholic Archbishop of Los Angeles to the Housing Authority had indeed occurred. I assumed the transfer change reflected the city's takeover of the property via eminent domain to make way for the proposed federal housing project. If this were the case then William Dubin could have been mistaken about McCrudden having anything to do with the Dodger Stadium deal. I began to think I had hit another dead end when the next entry on the list caught my eye. I saw a similar parcel number indicating it would be in the same map book. The transfer of title occurred in 1952, but this time between the Roman Catholic Archbishop of Los Angeles and the Gateway Real Estate Limited Liability Company. Among shelves of cataloged books I found the one with the parcel map of *El Santo Niño* and adjacent properties. From what I could see McCrudden may not have sold the *El Santo Niño* chapel property, but he did sell a parcel to Gateway that was next door.

"Thought I'd come by and check on you. Harriett asked me to take good care of you. Are you finding everything you need?"

Like Harriett, Shirley was a handsome woman and her bright pink-red lipstick brightened the nondescript work surroundings.

"Thanks, Shirley. I've made some progress, but I'm hoping you can help me with another search. Would it be possible to get the sale history, starting in 1952, for two pieces of property?"

"I can do that, just write down the addresses."

I quickly wrote down the two Chávez Ravine addresses and while I waited for Shirley to return I scanned the list for any other properties with a connection to Gateway. Now that I had something tangible, it took no time to find that needle in a haystack: a single property with a title transfer in 1962 between the Roman Catholic Archbishop of Los Angeles and Gateway. The most interesting thing about the find was that the property was located in the 4000 block of Hammel Street, north of Belvedere Park.

Shirley returned. "Here you go."

I didn't expect to see what Shirley showed me. "Wow, the Archdiocese only received $2800 for the sale of the chapel to the Housing Authority in 1952. I'm confused by what's noted for 1955 though."

"What's noted is a bit of shady history. In 1952 your chapel property became part of a larger 169 acre parcel sold to the Housing Authority for slightly over five million dollars; the Archdiocese received $2800 for its share. This same large parcel that included the chapel site sold again in 1955 to the City of Los Angeles, but this time for just over one million dollars."

"Wait, that doesn't add up."

"You're right. Smells rotten, doesn't it? When the Housing Authority sold the property to the City in 1955 they only recouped about six hundred dollars for their $2800 investment on that chapel property alone. We the tax payers were taken for a ride on that one."

"How was that allowed?"

"If I remember correctly, Congress authorized the Housing Authority to sell the large parcel with the provision that the City use the land for an appropriate public purpose."

"But how could Dodger Stadium be considered a public purpose?"

"Sugar, you're young. Excuse my candor, but there aren't enough orifices in one human body to accommodate all the people who will simultaneously try to screw you over in this life."

"I guess you're right."

"I know I'm right. Take a look at that other property you asked me to check. In 1952, the property was sold to

Gateway for $1000 and then Gateway turns around and sells it to the City in 1955 for one million. That's some kind of property appreciation."

"Now I'm really lost. The chapel property depreciates and this other adjacent property appreciates? It doesn't make sense."

"Sugar, once you add on a few more years to that young life of yours, you won't be surprised by the thievery in this world. Eventually the City deeded your two properties that were part of that large 169 acre parcel to O'Malley in exchange for no money."

"No money?"

"That's right. In fact, the City paid to grade the land and the County paid to create new access roads. For his part, O'Malley consented to build a public park but that never happened. He got away with just building his precious stadium."

"And I suppose O'Malley initially agreed to build the public park to qualify the deal as serving an appropriate public purpose?"

"You're catching on quick. It's easy to see the greed when you start to look."

Chapter 15
PLACE OF FELLOWSHIP

I couldn't sleep. There was no point. In three hours the surgeon would start to cut my *Tía's* flesh. Pieces of breast meat would be sliced and placed in a disposal pan destined for an incinerator. The thought haunted me. By dawn's break I found refuge in my car, *Azulita*. Her cocoon offered me temporary protection from the reality that nothing is permanent. I drove aimlessly until I came to rest across from Our Lady Queen of Angels. Without much thought, I opened the car door and walked into the church. I found the sanctuary empty like the night it offered me refuge when Ashworth's men were bent on finding and killing me.

I took a seat in the front pew. Jesus' near naked body was hanging above the altar nailed to a cross. The glossy statue of his mother, Mary, stood off to the right. Mary did not come to life as she had in a dream during my previous visit, when she told me that political retribution led to her son's crucifixion; his simple message of love and compassion stoked fear in those who held the reins of power. She told me not much had changed since the year 33: the powerful were still manipulating the masses. Mary had pointed to the iconic image of her son nailed to the cross as proof. If the church really cared about spreading His message, a more befitting image would show Him washing the feet of a stranger, she explained. Can you imagine, she had asked, if we all embraced each other with love? I couldn't imagine, but I wanted to.

Even though my brain told me nothing or no one could intervene to keep Carmen alive, I looked up at Jesus wanting to believe in the power of prayer. My reason was simple. I selfishly wanted more time with Carmen before I had to say goodbye.

§§§§§§§

When I arrived at the hospital Rocky and Sumire were about to leave.

Rocky whispered, "Hello Sweetheart. She's been asleep since we got here. You just missed Jaime."

"Have you seen the doctor?"

"We did, and he said that she's doing well. He thinks

they were able to get all the cancer and she should be able to go home in a couple of days."

Through tears I cried out "I can't believe it! That's great news, Rocky."

"She's going to be okay. She's not going anywhere, Alejandra."

"Meow."

Bewildered I asked, "Where's that coming from?"

Calmly Sumire answered, "Gato insisted on coming." Sumire opened up her knapsack to reveal the head of her handsome black cat.

"How long are all of you staying?" I asked.

Rocky answered, "We were getting ready to leave. Thought we'd go for an early lunch. Want to join us? There's not much you can do here. She needs her rest. The doctor thinks she'll be asleep most of the day."

"I'll go with you. I haven't eaten yet."

Sumire offered some advice. "The body must be cherished."

After filling up on oil soaked bags of fried shrimp from Johnny's Shrimp Boat at 2nd and Main, I told Rocky about my latest findings.

"Your friend William Dubin was partially right. It looks like McCrudden did sell a property to Clay Whitman, but it wasn't the church property. It was an adjacent parcel. But here's where it gets interesting. McCrudden sold it cheap and after a short time Whitman re-sold it to the City for quite a pretty penny."

"Interesting indeed. If the property was worth what the City paid then why didn't McCrudden want to get more for his Archdiocese?"

"We're on the same page. I found another property that McCrudden sold to Whitman back in 1962. You and Sumire want to go with me to check it out? It's close to Belvedere Park on Hammel Street?"

Sumire answered first. "Gato and me are in."

Rocky followed, "Me, too."

§§§§§§

We arrived at the address to find a shuttered run-down church. A chain link fence surrounded the property and the only way in was through a padlocked gate.

"Rocky can you work your magic and open this lock?"

"Step aside Sweetheart, I have the perfect tool for the job right here in my wallet."

Rocky pulled out a long and slender metal pick and set to work. After some effort he had us inside the gated yard and then he worked his pick again to get us into the church.

Sumire was the first to comment. "Don't they call this trespassing?"

"Only if we get caught." I responded.

Rocky added his opinion. "By the looks of things there's not much to trespass. This place is a mess."

Statues of saints lay tumbled over and broken on the floor. Church pews were covered with dust and cobwebs hung from the rafters. As we made our way toward the sanctuary a loud screeching whine pierced our ears. It was Gato. Sumire spoke what we all knew. "Gato senses something wrong."

We followed Gato's cry to a small room located off to the side of the altar and found the feline feverishly clawing at a locked door. Rocky set his pick to work. When the door opened we walked onto a small landing overlooking what appeared to be a dark cellar space. Gato immediately sped down a rickety wooden staircase and we followed with trepidation. At the bottom Rocky pulled a long string connected to a light bulb to take us out of the darkness. The light revealed a bed cot and strewn clothes across the floor. Food wrappers, a jug with water, and a bucket with human waste suggested the place had been recently inhabited.

In a whisper Sumire summed up the scene. "This is no place for living."

From across the room Gato screeched again. We followed the sound of his whine to a corner of the room.

Rocky was the first to voice what we all saw. "She's dead. It looks recent."

"How do you know?" I asked.

Rocky shined his pen light on the body. "No bloating, no smell. Look at the wound where that thin blade is sticking through her chest. The edges are still swollen and red. The war taught me more than I wanted to know about death."

I didn't waste any time. "I'm going to call the police."

Within minutes of placing the call a law enforcement team arrived and an hour later Lt. Smitz and Detective Carr showed up on the scene.

Smitz spotted me and walked over while Detective

Carr passed me as if I didn't exist. "Alejandra Marisol, why am I not surprised? I understand you told dispatch this scene is related to the Belvedere Park murders. What have you found?"

"The scene will speak for itself, Lieutenant."

"Not even going to give me a preview?"

"One dead woman. Looks like she died from a stab wound."

"Quite a find. And how did you come onto this place?"

"Well, that's a long story."

"Of course it is. I've got time to listen, but I guess the person you need to tell is Carr."

Smitz walked toward Carr and motioned for me to follow. "Detective, I'm sure you'll find what Alejandra has to say informative."

Detective Carr snapped back, "Really, Lieutenant?"

"Yes, really. I will pull rank this time."

Detective Carr relented and slowly walked over to me. "Okay, what can you tell me?"

"First, you need to get in touch with the person who owns this place."

"I've already spoken to Mr. Whitman."

"What did he say?"

"He's on his way down here. He sounded pretty shocked when I told him what you reported."

"Seems interesting that you'd call him before investigating the scene for yourself. Why would you take my report over the phone seriously?"

"Is there some reason I should think you'd lie?"

"No."

"Good. After finding out Whitman owned this place, I called him because I like efficiency. I like to get my cases cleared quickly."

I countered, "I think this case is going to be an exception. The scene you'll find in the cellar is tied to the Belvedere Park murders."

"Unless you have concrete evidence I'll be the judge of that. Tell me, Miss Marisol, how did you find this place?"

"I found it by making a connection to the previous owner of this place, the Catholic Archdiocese."

Carr laughed, "Let me guess, next thing you're going to tell me is that a priest committed the murder. No, no, how about a nun?"

"Look, I'm here, aren't I? It might be worthwhile to

question Whitman and Cardinal McCrudden about their financial relationship."

"Because you think a financial transaction leads to the formation of a murderous partnership? You're really grasping."

"You don't even think it's worth investigating?"

"I live in a world of facts, not make believe."

"This isn't make believe."

"I'm sure once Whitman gets here we'll have some answers."

Carr turned away from me and toward a patrol officer who tapped him on his shoulder. "Detective, Clay Whitman is here to see you."

"Show him over."

Clay Whitman wore his wealth. Dressed in a three-piece suit and sporting a gold ring with a nugget large enough to choke on, he took long confident strides toward us.

"Hello, Detective. Clay Whitman at your service. I got here as soon as I could. What you briefly told me sounds absolutely horrible. Are there any new details?"

"The investigation is really just starting. In fact, I

have yet to see the scene. Miss Marisol with the *LA Times* is the one who made the discovery."

Whitman turned toward me. He looked at me through cold blue-grey eyes as if he knew me. "Miss Marisol, let me take the liberty of thanking you for your efforts here today. I think it goes without saying that if you hadn't made this discovery the poor soul found here would not have been given a respectful resting place. But I must ask, do you make it a habit of trespassing onto other people's property?"

"No, I don't Mr. Whitman."

"Good to know. Given the good work Miss Marisol has done here today I assume we can forego pressing any charges. Is that correct, Detective?"

"Yes, Mr. Whitman. Thank you for your understanding. I am sure Miss Marisol is quite contrite. Isn't that right, Miss Marisol?"

I couldn't believe what I was hearing, but I had to agree . "Yes, that's right."

Detective Carr wasn't finished. "Good. Now if you will please excuse us."

I was furious, but there was nothing I could do. I turned to walk away but I moved slowly straining to hear the conversation between Carr and Whitman.

"So, Mr. Whitman, what can you tell me about this building?"

"I purchased this place about ten years ago. I had plans to tear down the church and construct an apartment building, but I haven't gotten around to it."

Carr noticed I hadn't taken my leave. He shot a smug look my way and walked Whitman in the opposite direction. For now I'd go quietly.

Chapter 16

POWERS THAT BE

The dank hot air focused my mind on images I didn't want to recall: the truck bed, the church cellar. I tried to focus on my driving but a wave of panic began to settle in my chest. The weight of my anxiety pulled tears from my eyes. It felt as if I were falling into quicksand. I took my eyes away from the road and wished I could stop time and melt into the sky's blue. Without warning my torso slammed up against my steering wheel as *Azulita* hit a curb. In one frantic motion I jerked the wheel to the left to pull back onto the street, but I over compensated and cut off the Helm's Bakery truck following close behind. The truck's back hatch flew open throwing trays of fresh baked goods into the air as the driver swerved and barely missed me. I pulled over and sat for a moment to settle down. I had nearly caused a serious accident as evidenced by the raspberry jelly donut splattered across my windshield. Even so, I was grateful for the distraction. It had calmed the pain. I merged back onto Broadway and continued toward the *Times* Building.

When I took my seat across from Harriett she wasted little time telling me the bad news. "I have to take you off the story. I should have never let you take the lead in the first place. I should have assigned our crime reporters to cover the Belvedere Park murders."

"But Harriett, I know the players. I know the back story here."

"I know."

"Why are you doing this?"

"I don't have a choice. This is coming from the top. Looks like a complaint has been brought against you. You trespassed onto private property."

"If I hadn't that latest victim would have never been discovered."

"Damn it, I don't have a choice. This is coming down from the top, the publisher, as in Otis Chandler. He doesn't like his reporters breaking the law for their stories. I warned you."

"You mean he doesn't like it when they get caught."

"You're right. Look, you should have called in your discovery of the body as an anonymous tip. Experience with this kind of thing would have taught you that much."

"This must be Clay Whitman's doing. He wants me off the case. Your friend at the County Clerk's Office helped me locate documents showing that McCrudden sold two pieces of property to Whitman. One located in Chávez Ravine and the other where we found that woman's body on Hammel Street."

"Damn, damn, damn." Harriett shook her head and looked at me stunned.

"Now it looks like we have a Cardinal and a rich developer potentially involved in a sex ring and murder. The pieces are here. I can't give up on this now."

"You're right, we've come too far to give into pressure."

I remembered my final question for William Dubin and asked a similar one. "Harriett, does Clay Whitman have a son?"

"That's a question out of left field. Why do you ask?"

"Gary Bell told his wife he was afraid the father and the son would be coming after him. I'm wondering if Bell was referring to Clay Whitman and his son."

"He used to have a son, a younger daughter too. Both were killed in a house fire when they were young."

"Harriett, how long ago?"

"About twenty years ago. It was tragic. It was in the news for days. I even remember the children's names, Robert and Roberta."

"I wish I knew what the father and the son meant to Gary Bell."

Harriett lit a cigarette. "I don't know, but first things first. Here's how we'll play it from here on out. Officially you'll be off the Belvedere Park story. I'll pass it off to someone else in Crime. I'll make sure they focus on the heinous nature of the murders, nothing more."

"What about Chandler? I don't want your job jeopardized."

"I'll take care of myself."

"Okay, I'll be in touch."

Chapter 17

IF AT FIRST YOU DON'T SUCCEED, TRY AGAIN

"Anything yet? Can you tell me anything about the woman found in the church cellar?"

"Interesting case. Come over."

Armand lifted the sheet to reveal the young corpse. She looked about my age, somewhere in her early twenties. Beyond the residual dirt that framed the outline of her cheeks and chin I saw a beautiful woman who even in death held my gaze as my eyes traced her soft brown skin.

Armand's voice jolted me back to the cutting reality that I wasn't standing at the foot of this woman's bed watching her sleep. I was looking at a murder victim, afforded no dignity, as she lay naked on a cold stainless steel table.

"Look right here. A thin blade was thrust under the xiphoid process at the bottom edge of the sternum. The person knew what he was doing because the blade was angled perfectly to pierce the heart. But that's not what makes the case interesting. Someone tried to kill her before she was stabbed to death."

"Huh?"

"I found a large concentration of a tocolytic drug in her system."

"What's that?"

"It suppresses contractions and that's why there was a large piece of the placenta still in her uterus."

"She was pregnant?"

"Yep, and I'd wager that the tocolytic was injected after she gave birth keeping the placenta from being fully released."

"How can you die from that?"

"If the placenta isn't completely discharged from the uterus the blood vessels inside continue to bleed and you hemorrhage to death. For some reason the drug didn't take full effect. Whoever killed her wasn't successful the first time and had to resort to another method."

"So where's the baby?"

"Maybe born dead or murdered too."

"We didn't find a dead baby. What if the baby was taken alive?"

Armand questioned, "But why would a killer want to deal with a live baby?"

"They'd deal with a live baby if it's seen as a commodity."

"What are you saying, Alejandra?"

"I think you know. It's too damn horrifying to speak out loud. It would be a perfect operation. There wouldn't be any need to try and coax a kid for your pleasure. You wouldn't have to run the risk of being caught kidnapping a child. You'd have a supply of anonymous babies. Babies that don't exist and can be easily disposed."

"And you think there are enough demons in this world to make such an operation worthwhile?"

"You know that best of all. You see the horrors, firsthand, right in this room."

"Well sure, but this is a whole other thing. It's sickening beyond belief and I sure hope there's some other explanation."

"Armand, what other explanation?"

"I don't know, but your idea is too unbelievable."

"I really hope you're right. Before I leave I'll need you to take a picture of this victim for me. It may come in handy."

Suddenly Olivia's voice boomed across the room. "*Primo*, I'm here."

Armand responded. "This is a surprise, I didn't expect you until later."

"I have a long incubation going for an experiment I'm running so I thought I'd come a little earlier."

"I have the blood sample on this latest female victim."

"Very good, *Primo*. I expect to have the DNA fingerprinting results completed on your first five victims, and this new one, within a day."

Olivia turned toward me. "Hello, Alejandra. Good to see you again."

"Nice to see you too. I hope your results will bring us closer to solving this case."

"More data can't hurt."

I questioned Olivia's words. Her previous results had hurt. Her data had brought us to see the vulnerability and innocence behind the faces of the men found slaughtered in the back of a truck. I now wondered what her new revelations would force me to see and endure.

Chapter 18

SAINT BASIL'S

Católicos Por La Raza, a coalition of Mexican-American Catholics, saw Saint Basil's Catholic Church as a gift to the affluent and a symbol of disregard for the poor. They couldn't reconcile constructing such an opulent structure at the cost of three million dollars while the Church did little to alleviate the plight of many who lived in substandard conditions.

This was my first visit, standing where *Católicos Por La Raza* had called on their sympathizers to gather for Midnight Mass on December 24th, 1969. The events of the evening didn't go well as more than 200 organized demonstrators pushed their way inside to chastise the Church. Cardinal McCrudden had begun the Christmas service when security officers, who were later joined by police, quelled the disturbance and returned order, but only after several protesters had been arrested.

Now here almost two years later, I recalled how McCrudden compared the protesters to the "rabble that gathered at the foot of the Cross when Christ died." Although I wasn't here to protest construction of a contemporary façade, I was here to see beyond the veneer. I needed answers that weren't visible from the outside.

As I gathered the nerve to knock on Saint Basil's rectory door Monsignor Crowe emerged. Before he could take a seat in his four door beige sedan I called out to him. "Monsignor, do you have a moment?"

Monsignor Crowe turned around to see me. Our eyes locked and I knew beyond any doubt he was the man in the Polaroid.

"Excuse me, do we know each other?"

"No Monsignor, we've never met. My name is Alejandra Marisol, I'm a reporter with the *Times*."

"What can I do for you?"

"We came across a photo we'd like to ask you about."

I wasn't about to show Crowe the photo for fear he'd take it from me and destroy it. Instead, I let a pointed description do the work. "It's a black and white Polaroid. It shows you on top of a woman. You're both naked. The woman's hands are tied to the bed frame."

Crowe was taken aback. His cheeks flushed and his eyes widened. He stood quiet but quickly regained his footing. It was obvious he didn't find himself on the defensive very often. He took aim and fired. "No such photo exists, not one with me in it."

I pushed back. "There's no mistake, it's you all right. Any comment before publication?"

"It isn't me and I'll deny it. Now if you'll excuse me, I have an important meeting to attend."

Crowe wasted little time driving away leaving me with nothing. I started to head back to my car when I noticed a gardener alongside the rectory cutting back the shrubbery. It was a long shot but worth pursuing.

"Hello, Sir."

"Yes."

"I have an appointment to meet the Monsignor."

"The Monsignor left. I don't know when he'll be back."

"Oh my, I'm sure he told me to be here at this time. I wonder if I got it wrong and I'm supposed to meet him somewhere else. Do you know where he went?"

"He has a lunch meeting every Wednesday at Clifton's."

"Can you tell me your name?"

"Romero."

"Romero, maybe you can help?"

Romero shot an affable look my way. "How?"

"I'm a social worker for a hospital. The large one close to downtown, LA County General."

"Yes, I know it."

"Over the phone I told the Monsignor I needed to find anyone who might know a woman admitted to the hospital. She arrived very sick and before she became unconscious she mentioned the Monsignor's name and Saint Basil's."

I passed the picture Armand took of the dead woman over to Romero. "Do you know her?"

"Itzel, that's her name. Will she be okay? She doesn't look good."

Romero was visibly upset, but I couldn't turn back now. I had the opening I needed. "Yes, we think she'll be okay. Can you tell me anything about her? Where we might be able to find her family?"

"She worked and lived here, but only for a little while. One day Monsignor took her away and she never came back."

"How long ago?"

"About a month."

"Do you know where the Monsignor took her?"

"I guess to a place to have her baby."

"She was pregnant?"

"Yes."

"Did she ever talk about the father of the baby?"

"No, but the Monsignor took care of her. He's a good man. He helps women like Itzel."

"And does the Monsignor always take the women away before they have their babies?"

"Yes, to a home for pregnant women."

"Do any of the women ever come back here?"

"No."

"Do you know where they go after they have their babies?"

"I think the Monsignor helps them get back to their families in Mexico."

Cynically, I asked, "Is that what the Monsignor told you?"

Romero's puzzled face told me I had overstepped. I quickly backtracked. "I meant to say how nice of the Monsignor to do that. I'm hoping the Monsignor will be able to help us find Itzel's family."

"You'll have to ask the Monsignor. I don't know."

"Is there anyone else who knew Itzel?"

"Lupe spent a little time with her. I'll take you to her."

Romero led me to the back of the rectory where we found two women preparing food in a large open kitchen. He walked over to the woman dicing onions. Of the two, she was the oldest and clearly not pregnant like her cooking partner who was busy stirring the contents of a large pot.

Romero called out to Lupe. "*Hola Lupe, esta señorita dice que tiene preguntas sobre Itzel y su familia. Ella dice que Itzel está en el hospital.*"

Even after hearing Itzel was in the hospital and that I came to see if she had family, Lupe stayed focused on her onions and kept her response to a few words. "*No tengo nada que decir.*"

She said she had nothing to say but I made another attempt, pleading directly with Lupe to tell me something about Itzel. "*¿Lupe, por favor, qué sabes de* Itzel?"

Lupe didn't budge. She shook her head and said nothing. I turned to the young pregnant woman in the room and asked if she knew Itzel. "*¿La conoces?*"

I could barely hear her response. "No."

Romero voiced the obvious. "We can't help you. Itzel wasn't here long."

I felt like the young woman was hiding something, but I didn't push. "Thanks for trying to help."

Before leaving I asked Romero to confirm that the number I had for the rectory was the best way to follow up with the Monsignor. After saying the Edison exchange Romero recited the numbers I used to reach St. Basil's. It was music to my ears and it cemented Eduardo Cuevas' connection to this place.

"Sure do love it when people use the phone exchanges." I said.

Romero added, "The Monsignor loves them too. He uses them all the time."

As Romero ushered me to the front door I could hear Lupe's words. "*Graciela, ve a la tienda y compra pan, del que le gusta al Monseñor.*" Lupe had asked Graciela to buy the Monsignor's favorite bread. I saw the request as my chance. I'd wait on the street for Graciela to return from the store and try my luck one more time. Eduardo Cuevas managed to leave the clue that brought me here, now I hoped mentioning his name to Graciela could bring me more.

I stood at the corner of Kingsley Drive and Wilshire Boulevard and waited. When I spotted Graciela I walked to meet her before she could turn into the rectory. I got ready to pull Eduardo Cuevas, literally, from my pocket. I handed Graciela the morgue photo of Eduardo Cuevas. "*¿Lo conoces?* Do you know him?"

The woman stared at the photo and remained silent. I pushed again. "*Por favor, si lo conoces, dime.* Please tell me if you know him."

Graciela shied away from me and didn't say a word.

I had to take a harder line. I told her to take a good look at the picture to see that Eduardo was dead. That he was murdered. I told her I had lied at the rectory. Itzel had also been murdered and that she would be next if she refused to talk to me.

I asked again, "*¿Conoces a* Eduardo Cuevas?"

Graciela stared at the ground while answering. "*Sí, lo conozco, pero no sabía su nombre.*" She'd seen him she said, but she didn't know his name.

How did she know him? "*¿Cómo lo conociste?*"

The young woman cried as she answered. "*Necesitaba dinero y una amiga me exigió hablar con él.*"

Graciela needed money and a friend told her to see Eduardo. I couldn't help but think the worst. I expected an answer I didn't want to hear. Regardless, I had to ask what kind of deal Eduardo made with Graciela. "*¿Qué es lo que tenías que hacer?*"

"*Tener un bebé.*"

Graciela had confirmed my fear. She would be paid to have a baby, but for whom? "*¿Y, para quién vas a tener el bebé?*"

"*Para una pareja que no puede tener su propio bebé.*"

Graciela's answer didn't align with the perverted and deranged path I had shared with Armand about Itzel. Even though I had heard of people being paid to have babies for infertile couples, I wasn't buying it, not in this case. Everything about Graciela's face indicated she believed what she told me. But if it were as simple as exchanging money for a baby then Itzel should still be alive. There had to be something else going on. Before leaving I had to confirm my suspicion and ask who fathered her baby? "*¿Quién es el padre de su bebé?*"

I handed her the photos of the four young men found murdered along with Eduardo Cuevas. Graciela pointed to one of them and began to sob. She told me she didn't know him but he treated her well. They each wanted the same thing: a better life for themselves and their families back in Mexico.

I asked one last question. "*¿El Monseñor te ha lastimado?*"

This time she looked me straight in the eye and answered in the few English words she could string together. "No hurt. *El Monseñor*, he a good man."

Chapter 19

JUST A PILE OF CRAP

The phone was ringing when I walked into my house. As soon as I answered Armand began to tell me about Olivia's DNA test results. I couldn't believe none of the five murdered men fathered Itzel's baby. If I assumed Graciela told me the truth about one of the murdered men fathering her child, then who had fathered Itzel's? With no one else to accuse I placed my bet on Monsignor Crowe. Even though I knew little about DNA testing, I was certain that a sample of the Monsignor's cells was needed.

The gardener, Romero, mentioned Crowe had a lunch date at Clifton's and that's where I needed to go. I wouldn't be able to approach Crowe though, not after our interaction. As luck would have it Rocky and Sumire were home and on board to help me get my sample.

On our way downtown Rocky offered up an idea. "Sumire and Gato will distract the Monsignor while I pickpocket him. I'll make sure to get something that'll have his cells, like a comb or handkerchief. What do you think?"

Sumire enthusiastically agreed to the plan. "Gato and I are ready."

"Here's a picture of him so you'll know what he looks like." I showed Rocky and Sumire the same recent article with Crowe's picture I had shown Harriett. "Once Sumire confirms Crowe is still inside, you'll both wait for him outside the restaurant. I'll park ahead. One last thing, make sure whatever you take from him gets placed in here."

I handed Rocky a small plastic bag. "We need a clean sample, one with only Crowe's cells. We have to limit the chance of any contaminating DNA from you and Sumire."

"Not my place to question." Rocky said.

I turned to Sumire. "How will you distract the Monsignor?"

Rocky interrupted to answer. "Shit out of luck."

"You're saying Sumire won't be able to distract him?" I asked.

"Shit out of luck. That's what I call my petrified poop." Rocky opened a paper bag to show us the contents.

"That's disgusting. Where did you get it and why do you still have it?"

"World War I. It's my good luck charm."

I shook my head. "I'd love to hear this one but right now we have to get going. Rocky, promise you'll tell me the story later."

"It's a promise."

I turned to Sumire. "How are you planning to use the poop?"

"I'll place it on the sidewalk and ask the Monsignor to hold Gato so I can clean it up."

I questioned the logic in her plan. "If you're planning to pretend this pile came from Gato there's no way Crowe will buy it. It's too big."

Sumire countered, "Won't matter. You'll see."

"Alejandra, I got to agree with Sumire. I'll get what I need before Crowe even realizes the pile can't possibly be Gato's. Remember, this is my lucky shit."

After Sumire confirmed Crowe was inside Clifton's, she placed the poop pile on the sidewalk. When Crowe exited the restaurant Sumire walked toward him with a leashed Gato at her side. I could hear the conversation from where I was parked. "Father, please can you help? Can you hold my cat? He couldn't wait."

Sumire pointed to the large mound on the ground.

Crowe paused and looked down. "That came from your cat?"

Before Sumire could muster an answer Rocky had brushed by the priest and kept walking ahead. From what I saw there was no way Rocky could get a sample from Crowe.

"My cat eats like a lion and poops like one too." Sumire announced.

Crowe took ahold of Gato's leash while Sumire scooped up the poop back into the brown paper bag. "Thank you very much, Father."

Once everyone made it back inside the car Rocky gave us the news. "Snatching the Padre's comb couldn't have been easier. And my petrified poop helped get the job done."

"So tell me, Rocky, how did you come across the poop?" I asked.

"We were involved in a large offensive in the Argonne Forest of France, close to the German border. We lost a lot of men there and I came damn close to being one of them. We were out of ammunition and surrounded on all sides. The only thing we could do was to build shallow bunkers, cover them with branches, hide there, and hope the Germans wouldn't see us. When the Germans came rolling through they noticed the misplaced branches covering up some of the bunkers. They shot through the branches and that's when I could hear my comrades screaming before they died."

"They didn't find your bunker?" I asked.

"They would have if it hadn't been for the wild boar that came out of nowhere. He walked right up to the edge of my bunker and stuck his large snout through some of the branches to look right at me. He must have weighed 500 pounds, maybe more. He stayed right there at the edge while the Germans advanced. Even with gunfire everywhere that boar didn't move. When the Germans got to the edge of my bunker they were so focused on that giant boar they missed my hiding place. I stayed in that bunker for a full day waiting for the Germans to clear the area. When I finally climbed out I found out why the boar didn't care about the German advance. He had been busy taking the biggest dump of shit, right there at the edge of my bunker. Just a couple feet away he lay dead. He paid the price for nature calling on him at such a bad time. No doubt about it. I got this shit out of luck and it saved my life. The combination of the light rain during the night and the gunpowder in the air managed to petrify it. So I took a pile as my charm and I've had it ever since."

I shook my head. "That's one crazy story."

Rocky looked down at the pile of petrified organic matter. "War's not pretty and this pile reminds me that nothing but shit comes from it."

"Let's drop off the comb with Armand so he can give it to his cousin for testing and then reward ourselves with a visit to see Carmen." I announced.

We took Gato's high pitched meow as a firm approval of the plan.

Chapter 20

BAIT AND HOOK

"I'm below 200, *M'ija*. Now that Ta is gone I'm seven pounds lighter. Proof you can find something good in almost anything."

"I'm just glad you're going to be okay, *Tía*."

"Doctor says I should be able to go home tomorrow."

Sumire couldn't keep her surprise a secret any longer. "I made new bras, special for you."

Carmen was thrilled. "I can't wait to see them. They're for the new one breasted me?"

"Yes, special for you." Sumire confirmed.

I added more details about Sumire's bra design. "Each bra has one falsie."

"I love it. A prosthetic boob to go with my prosthetic leg. So tell me, how have you all been since I've been laid up in here?"

I answered. "Still trying to get a break in the case. Rocky and Sumire have been a big help."

"Wish I could help you too."

"I know you do, *Tía*."

"What do you know so far, *M'ija*?"

"One thing I'm pretty certain about, I think Cardinal McCrudden is somehow involved."

"Oh *M'ija*, that's too much. Give me the scoop."

"Remember the phone number I dialed using the exchange?"

"Sure, the number was disconnected."

"That's because one of my numbers was wrong. When I redialed using the right number I reached St. Basil's rectory. The Cardinal's right-hand man, Monsignor Crowe, lives there. He's the man in a photo I found at Ashworth's house. Crowe is having sex with a woman tied to a bed in that photo, and I think the Cardinal was blackmailed to keep the photo from going public."

"Shit. The Cardinal? Then it's more like Holy Shit, right *M'ija*?"

"You have a point," I said. "I just know that photo is tied to the victims found at Belvedere Park and to Ashworth's child sex trade."

"What are you going to do now, *M'ija*?"

"I'm not sure. It's not like I can call the Cardinal and

ask him if he was blackmailed."

"Why not? Go ahead and call him on the phone. What's the worst that can happen? He hangs up on you?"

Rocky agreed. "Men with power don't reveal their hand so easily; hanging up would show he's rattled. He won't do that."

"Okay, I'll play it your way. Rocky, do you think your friend William Dubin can get me the Cardinal's phone number?"

"I'm sure of it. I'll call him right now."

I followed Rocky to the public pay phone in the hall. After he got me the Cardinal's number I placed the call and the line connected. "His Eminence, Cardinal McCrudden's residence."

"Good afternoon, my name is Alejandra Marisol. I'm calling from the *LA Times*. I'm hoping to get a comment from the Cardinal regarding a story related to the Archdiocese I'm preparing to write."

"A story regarding what, specifically?"

"It's a sensitive issue so I'd like to speak with the Cardinal directly about it."

"Your name again?"

"Alejandra Marisol."

"One moment."

My heart pounded with nervous anticipation but it didn't have to wait long. "Cardinal McCrudden speaking."

"Thank you, Cardinal, for taking my call. My name is Alejandra Marisol. I'm a reporter with the *LA Times*."

"Yes, how can I help you?"

I didn't beat around the bush. "We've come across a photograph showing Monsignor Crowe in a compromising situation."

"Compromising in what way?"

"The photo is of a sexual nature. Before we go public we're asking for you to comment."

"I'm not making any comment about a photograph you have not shown me."

"So you're not surprised that a photo like the one I've described exists."

I had stoked the embers. "What are you trying to do? How dare you twist my words? Is the *Times* now nothing more than a cheap tabloid?"

I couldn't wait. I had to feed him a larger piece of bait while I had him on the phone. "It's not just the photograph.

We have evidence Monsignor Crowe is involved in a sex trade operation."

"I don't know who's feeding you these lies, but if you print one word of it I'll hold you liable."

He was calling my bluff. "That's fine, Cardinal. I hoped you'd speak to me before the evidence is turned over to the police."

"I want to see this evidence before I say anything."

"When and where?"

"There will be a gala fundraiser for the Archdiocese tonight at the Biltmore Hotel. You can meet me there."

"Not sure that's such a good idea. There will be a lot of people, including the Monsignor I assume."

"Monsignor Crowe will not attend. We'll have our privacy. I'll have meetings with donors throughout the night in a hotel room I have reserved. You can be my last appointment at 11:00pm."

"That will be fine."

"Very well. I'll be in room 916."

Chapter 21

GEISHA SLEUTH

My first challenge, what to wear? I stood in front of my modest closet to see a single dress. It was the one I wore to my mom's funeral. I couldn't bear to wear it again. On the off chance Sumire had something I could borrow, I headed across the path to her unit. As I approached I found her rolled out on an exercise mat.

"Sumire, what are you up to?"

"Getting ready for my Jujutsu martial art meet next week. I'm practicing moves."

"I hate to bother you, but I'm hoping you might have something on the fancy side I can wear tonight."

"Fancy, no. I have nothing like that." Sumire paused. "Wait, maybe I have something. Follow me."

From the back of her closet Sumire brought out a large box. "I think this could work."

Sumire opened the box to reveal a black kimono with large red and white flowers. While the garment was beautiful, it didn't fit what I had in mind. "Uh thanks, but this is too nice for me to wear."

"Please, you take it. It belonged to my mother. If she were alive she would want you to wear it."

I didn't want to hurt Sumire's feelings, but I had to say it. "This style isn't right for me."

Sumire wouldn't take no for an answer. "I will fix it. It won't take long."

Sumire reached back into her closet and this time pulled out her sewing machine. She could see the concern on my face. "Don't worry, it will look good. I'm going to make it fit the times. You can help."

For the next hour I cut fabric as Sumire threaded her bobbin and stitched new seams. When finished she had created what she described as a mini midi. The asymmetrical pattern boasted a formfitting mini skirt on one side and a draping midi that flared just above the knee on the other. The waistline and sleeves of the kimono were drawn in tight for a tapered look.

"It's ready for you to try."

I put it on and loved it. I felt chic and elegant. "Sumire, what do you think about shoes?"

"Knee-high black boots. Where are you going?"

"I need to meet a priest, a high ranking one. He's hiding something and I need to find out what it is."

"Truth doesn't stay hidden. Like a white grub hatched from a buried egg; it eventually worms its way above ground."

"I hope the truth makes it to the surface before someone tries to bury me."

"You shouldn't go alone. I will come with you."

"Thanks, Sumire, but an LAPD captain is going to meet me there. He'll make sure I stay safe."

"Good."

§§§§§§

I had never seen anything like the Biltmore Hotel. Frescos, murals, embroidered tapestries, and other wondrous treasures were everywhere I turned. The closest I'd ever gotten to this kind of posh elegance was when my mom took me "play shopping," as she called it. One of our favorite destinations was Bullock's Department Store. Its white marbled walls and ornate deco design would transport me into a world of pageantry. I saw nothing imaginary about my world right now. Everything in my sight was real, including the tall commanding figure who brushed by me dressed in a cassock that reached to the ground. It was Cardinal McCrudden and he walked with a confidence I imagined only came from thinking you had a direct connection to God.

I followed him from a safe distance into the Crystal Ballroom. The palatial space boasted an arcade of arched windows that were outlined with lush baroque draperies. Sconces anchored onto columns bounced ambient lighting off the walls and overhead chandeliers eliminated any shadows where I could hide. My outfit had caught the attention of several in attendance, one of whom walked toward me.

"Mr. Whitman."

"Ah, Miss Marisol. You're the last person I expected to see."

"I could say the same thing about you."

"I happen to be a big supporter of the Cardinal's. He has a real vision, not only for knowing what's needed to prepare our soul for salvation, but also for the political structure that's needed to feed and sustain the Church."

"Interesting perspective. Somehow I didn't take you for a man of God."

"God lives in us all. So tell me, Miss Marisol, what brings you to the Biltmore? I trust they let you in the door and you didn't have to break in. Are you here looking for a dead body? Under the table perhaps?"

"Don't you care about the murdered woman found on your property?"

"Oh, I care immensely. I also care about the sanctity of property rights."

"You talk about your property as if its worth were equal to a human life."

"I'm sorry about the woman who was found dead, and I'm sure Detective Carr will find who's responsible."

"You made sure I'm no longer involved."

"I made a call to an old friend about your misconduct, and he, not I, took you off the story."

"It appears you have a lot of important friends such as Cardinal McCrudden and Otis Chandler. I'm sure the list is quite long."

"Friends are always an important resource. One should not take them for granted. You never know when you might need to call on one for help. Take you and me for example."

I couldn't believe what I heard. "You and I. Are we friends?"

"We could be. The circumstances of how we met were, I admit, a bit strained. I don't like to ever give up on an opportunity to make a new friend."

Clay Whitman pulled out a business card from his jacket pocket and handed it to me. "Should you ever find yourself jobless you may need me. I employ a large number of women like you who were born to clean the mess others leave behind."

I wanted to spit on his card and throw it in his face. "Men like you are blinded by your own power. You won't be prepared for what's coming."

"What could you possibly be talking about?"

"The wretched of the earth, Mr. Whitman. Those you have exploited and manipulated. When they realize their power and take you down. It won't be pretty. It will be downright ugly."

I didn't wait for Clay Whitman to respond. I went to the bar and ordered a shot of Crown Royal on the rocks.

Halfway through my drink my rage started to subside. It was 10:30, and I expected Captain Allen to arrive at any moment. I lifted my glass to take another drink when I felt someone slide into the empty seat next to me. Before I could turn to see who it was, a man's voice offered up an apology. "I'm sorry you had to experience that."

I rotated to see the man now sitting to my left. His chiseled good looks and seductive smile sent an involuntary ripple through my body. I chalked it up to the alcohol and responded by tightly crossing my legs, hoping to quash the wave of arousal. He continued. "I overheard a little bit of that conversation back there. Mr. Whitman can be a bastard." The man took a sip of his drink. "How rude of me to interrupt you and not introduce myself. I'm Bob Dennon and you are?"

With my composure slightly regained, I replied. "Alejandra Marisol."

"Can I get you another drink?"

"Still working on this one, but thank you."

"What brings you here tonight? You don't fit the profile of the typical Archdiocese supporter."

"How's that?"

The slur in Bob Dennon's voice told me the alcohol in his blood had loosened his inhibitions. "Take a look around. Do you see any other women that even remotely look like you?"

I was taken aback. The look of incredulity upon my face couldn't be missed.

Bob Dennon chuckled and his mouth broke into a wide smile. "I only mean that in the most complimentary way. Look at these stodgy women. The stoles they're wearing look more alive than they do. Allow me to say that dress fits you quite nicely."

I relented. "I accept the compliment. And you're right. I'm not here to help the Archdiocese raise money. I'm here working for the *Times*."

"A reporter? Is that how you met Mr. Whitman, covering a story?"

"I guess you could say that. How do you know him?"

"One of his henchmen. There are a few like me here tonight. We look for investors for capital projects that Mr. Whitman's company oversees."

"And the Archdiocese is involved in some of these projects?"

"It's no secret. Mr. Whitman and the Archdiocese have a good working relationship."

"Relationship, is that what it's called?"

"Let's just say Mr. Whitman has his hands in a lot of different deals and the Archdiocese is one of them."

Bob Dennon turned toward the center of the ballroom and then continued. "All these rich people are aching to dole out their money, especially when they know their investments will get them even more cash in the end."

Bob Dennon had my full attention. "How does investing in the Archdiocese make money?"

"I'm not at liberty to discuss financial strategies. Suffice it to say that wealth begets wealth."

"So it literally does pay to have a powerful friend like the Cardinal?"

"Yes. Friends like the Cardinal and his ruthless sidekick, Monsignor Crowe, are good to have."

Bob Dennon mentioned the name of the man I wanted to know more about. "Should I assume you don't like the Monsignor?"

Bob Dennon moved in closer and whispered. "I like you. Can I tell you something, just between you and me?"

I didn't know where Bob Dennon was going. "Of course."

"One has to be ruthless when it comes to making money. I don't fault the Monsignor for that. But there is something not right about him."

I wanted to ask Bob Dennon if he thought Crowe could be capable of impregnating women, murdering them, and selling their babies. "What do you mean, not right?"

"Don't listen to me, I've had too much to drink. What do you say we get out of here and go some place where we can get a decent meal? I sure could use a good martini and a steak. Have you ever been to the Pacific Dining Car on 6th?"

"Thanks, but I need to stay. I'm scheduled to meet the Cardinal."

"Face to face with the man of the hour. Well, I hope you get what you need from him. It was nice meeting you. I have a feeling we'll cross paths again. I look forward to seeing you then."

"You're a bit presumptuous, Mr. Dennon."

"Oh please, we've shared time over a drink. First

names from here on out, Alejandra."

"Okay. Nice to meet you, Bob."

Bob left me as I finished my last sip of courage now coating two melting ice cubes at the bottom of my glass. Captain Allen was nowhere in sight. With or without him the time had come to meet the Cardinal for a high stakes winner take all game, and I was ready to play my best poker yet.

§§§§§§§

When I exited the elevator on the 9th floor there was no one in sight. I took a slow deliberate walk to my destination, Room 916. I knocked. The door slowly opened and I stepped inside. McCrudden closed the door behind me.

"You're on time. Please have a seat, Miss Marisol."

I took a seat at a small table near the window and Cardinal McCrudden sat across from me. Without any prompting, McCrudden spoke first. "When I arrived in Los Angeles in 1948 to head this great diocese I saw the city before me like an open landscape. I immediately set to work erecting new parishes and schools; each built with the purpose of giving glory to our Almighty Father in Heaven. It is a legacy I am proud to honor with my continued service to God and his people." The Cardinal reached for his crucifix. "I know about the picture you are here to show me. Monsignor Crowe's indiscretion has weighed on my soul for a long time, but he has found his way back to the Lord. His early stumble is far behind him. We all falter, Miss Marisol. This is the reason I have stood by Monsignor Crowe and will continue to do so. He is a good man."

"That's the second time I've heard Monsignor Crowe referred to as a good man, but do good men prey on the weaknesses of immigrants? Do good men sell children for sex?"

"You're like a cannon without a cannonball, Miss Marisol. You might be able to scare people with the size of your weapon but without ammunition you can't inflict any damage."

"And you don't think the photo of Monsignor Crowe is ammunition?"

"By itself, no. You have nothing else because Monsignor Crowe's only misstep is seen in that photograph."

"If you truly believe the photo poses no real threat why did you agree to meet with me?"

"Do not mistake my words, Miss Marisol. I would be remiss if I told you I did not care if the photo went public. Such a depiction of Monsignor Crowe would certainly strike a blow against the Church's image and standing. Our enemies, and there are many, would relish in the untold political and social ramifications such a revelation would bring. I asked you here to tonight to try to convince you that Monsignor Crowe is not involved in selling children for sex. Your allegations are simply not true."

"I'm listening. Convince me."

"It is you who needs to convince me. Besides the photo what else do you have?"

"A few days ago five men were found dead in the back of a pickup truck. One of those men etched a phone number into his leather belt just before he was murdered. That phone number belongs to the rectory at St. Basil's."

Cardinal McCrudden rose out of his seat and poured two glasses of water and handed one to me. "Please continue."

"When I went to the rectory I met a pregnant woman,

a Mexican immigrant. She was being paid to have a baby, and the father of that baby is one of the dead men found in the truck. I know there was another pregnant woman, by the name of Itzel, who worked at the rectory. The gardener told me the Monsignor took Itzel away to have her baby. We found Itzel murdered in a cellar of an abandoned church that the Archdiocese used to own."

The Cardinal showed no emotion.

I pressed. "Did you hear what I said?"

The Cardinal calmly continued. "Some years back I was approached, much like your call yesterday, telling me about the same photograph with Monsignor Crowe. At that time the Monsignor hadn't been a parish priest for more than a couple of years. I barely started to build the framework needed to grow the diocese when I received a phone call."

"Who was it?"

The Cardinal ignored my question. "Whoever seeks to keep his life will lose it, but whoever loses his life for My sake, he is the one who will save it."

Impatiently I asked, "What are you talking about?"

I could barely hear the Cardinal mumble. "Luke 9:24."

The Cardinal turned abruptly and held the crucifix out toward me as if I were a vampire whose flesh he needed to burn. "My Lord gave His life, the ultimate sacrifice so that we may one day join Him in Heaven. In His light I have given my life over to the people of this city. I have tried to reach as many souls as I could. I had hoped they would come to know our Lord and open their heart to His glory."

I snapped back. "That is not a justification! I know you sold the church property where Itzel's body was found and a parcel of land in Chávez Ravine to Clay Whitman. I'm guessing you did it to keep Crowe's dirty deed a secret."

Cardinal McCrudden walked over to the window. "I like this room, especially during the day. From this spot I can watch the birds fly in and out of the trees at Pershing Square. So many different species have to live together and they do. There's an order to it."

I couldn't imagine what the Cardinal meant.

"Miss Marisol, what do you think would happen if we erected a birdhouse with food inside and permitted only one bird species to enter?"

"I don't know."

"I will tell you. Disorder would occur. The birds that

could gain entry would grow fat and lazy and become reliant on help. The other birds that couldn't get inside would grow envious and ultimately destroy the birdhouse. Communism is a real threat. Housing projects only breed entitlement and entitlement is the fodder of secularism. Hard work and self-reliance are God-given virtues that we must not turn our back upon."

"Keeping with your model, if every species were allowed to get inside the birdhouse that could solve the problem. In any case, I don't know what birdhouses and communism have to do with Monsignor Crowe. Admit it. You sold the land to Clay Whitman to protect Crowe."

"You have no right to come here and make false accusations. If it had not been for Clay Whitman, communism would have taken deeper root in this city."

"Oh yes. You thought the slated housing project, Elysian Park Heights, was part of a communist plot."

From the side bedroom a voice boomed. "It was."

I turned to see Monsignor Crowe in the doorway. "You've been here the whole time?" It sounded as if I had asked a question, but it was a statement of fact.

Crowe answered. "Yes. I am here at the Cardinal's

request. He asked that I try to convince you I am only guilty of losing sight of my Lord with the woman in the photograph."

"Why are you admitting this now? Why didn't you tell me this when I asked you earlier?"

"I wanted to consult the Cardinal."

"What about Itzel and Graciela? How do you explain them?"

Crowe turned away from me and looked at the Cardinal.

I lost patience. "Don't turn to him. Answer my question. If you're innocent tell me what you know about Itzel and Graciela."

Crowe sat down. "I thought I was helping the women."

"Helping them how? To make money in exchange for a baby?"

Crowe came to his feet. "Yes, the women who came to me were desperate. We, I mean I, didn't see anything wrong with helping them and a family who wanted a baby."

"We? Who's the we?"

Crowe hesitated. "A man named Eduardo Cuevas asked me to help."

"How did you meet him?"

"He attends church at St. Basil's."

"Attends?" I asked.

"Yes, he's usually at the 11:00 service."

"Are you telling me you don't know Eduardo Cuevas is dead?"

"What? When?"

"He was found brutally murdered along with four other men."

"Oh my dear, Lord."

"So you didn't know about Eduardo's murder?"

"I had no idea." Crowe sunk his head into his hands.

"And what about Itzel, Monsignor. You didn't know about her murder either? She was found stabbed. Looks as if it happened shortly after she gave birth."

"I didn't know." Crowe asked with urgency. "What about the baby?"

"There was no sign of a baby."

Crowe pressed again. "Did you talk to anyone from Angel of Mercy? Maybe they know something."

"What's Angel of Mercy?"

"That's where I took Itzel. It's a home for unwed mothers."

The Cardinal who had been quiet now broke into the conversation. "I hope you will drop your course of persecution against Monsignor Crowe. I am prepared to deal with the repercussions if you make the photograph public, but I daresay you won't be."

Had the Cardinal just threatened me? "What do you mean by that?"

"You are young and naïve, Miss Marisol. I am trying to help you before fate catches up with you and I will be helpless to stand in its way. All you have is a photograph, nothing more."

I played my last card. "Do you appreciate the power of science, Cardinal?"

"Now it's my turn. What do you mean, Miss Marisol?"

"Science can be used to reveal the truth. Science can tell us who impregnated the woman found dead in the church cellar."

I turned toward Crowe. "If what you're telling me is correct then science will verify it."

Crowe remained silent, but not the Cardinal. "I am a man of faith, Miss Marisol. That is the only truth I need. I trust you can find your way to the door."

"Yes, of course."

As I closed the door behind me I realized I had been out of my league. My best game had been child's play for the Cardinal.

Chapter 22

GOING DOWN

Unless Olivia's test results could link Crowe to Itzel's baby, I had nothing to tie him to her murder. Was the Cardinal right? Had the Monsignor only been guilty of a sexual indiscretion? A loud ding sounded the elevator's arrival. As I made my descent to the lobby I knew my first order of business; call Armand to see if the DNA results were in. I used the reflection of the elevator's metal pushbutton pad to apply a new coat of lipstick. When I finished, the elevator stopped and the doors opened to the fifth floor.

"Alejandra Marisol, what a surprise."

"Bob, I thought you'd be enjoying a martini and steak by now."

"My plan changed when I met a potential client. How did your meeting with His Eminence turn out?"

"Not as productive as I had hoped."

"Sorry to hear that."

As Bob Dennon moved into the carriage his foot appeared to get caught in the grate of the doorway.

"Damn, my heel is stuck."

I bent down to try and help. Bob reacted to my gesture. He quickly placed his hand over my face and tightly pressed a damp cloth against my mouth and nose. I tried to fight. The fumes from a strong solvent reached their way up my nasal passages and left me defenseless as he dragged me out of the elevator and into a room across the hall. I heard the door close and then everything went black.

§§§§§§§

My eyes strained to focus. What had just happened? I instinctively moved to stand, but couldn't. My arms and legs were tightly bound against a wooden chair. Seconds passed before it came back to me. Bob Dennon had knocked me out with some sort of chemical, chloroform, I'd guess. How Dennon fit into the puzzle I didn't know and it really didn't matter. I had to figure out a way to get free and be quick about it.

I tried to think clearly, but the throbbing pain in my head and the taped cloth stuffed in my mouth didn't help. I struggled to breathe and soon found myself in a state of terror. Hope was slipping away. Through my tears, a vision of my mom appeared. She kept her distance and didn't say a word, but I could see her love for me in her eyes. It was a familiar expression, one I remembered from my childhood. Today, as in the past, it filled me with strength and freed me from self-doubt. As quickly as she appeared she was gone and I didn't hesitate to use the courage she brought me. I rocked the chair from side to side using the momentum to move to a window covered by a heavy drape. When I made it, I rocked one more time knocking the chair into the glass. The drape, as I had hoped, kept the glass from slicing into my flesh as it splintered.

Now that I had broken the window what could I do? The window stood too high to try and use the shards to cut away the ropes binding my arms and hands. My best option was to use a hanging shard to cut away the tape across my mouth. I tipped my chair, relying on the sill to hold me at a 30 degree angle as I used a pointed edge of glass to cut through the tape. Within a few seconds I was able to spit out the gag, but my upper lip had paid the price. I felt the taste of warm blood running into my mouth as I heard a key enter the lock. I pushed my head through the window hoping to catch sight of a passerby from five floors above the ground, but no luck. Before Bob Dennon pulled me away from the window I lapped up a broken shard of glass.

Dennon grabbed my chair and dragged it to the middle of the room. "Ashworth was right. You have a lot of fight."

I didn't respond. I couldn't. I had to focus on not swallowing the sharp object resting on my tongue.

"Nothing to say. No questions to ask?"

I gave him a blank stare.

"That's okay, Alejandra. I'll look forward to hearing your sweet moan when I start to peel the first bit of skin away from the fascia. That's usually when it starts: the begging. And don't think anyone will hear you. I made sure to reserve the rooms next door and across the hall. We'll have lots of privacy, you and me.

Dennon rolled out sheets of plastic onto the floor and discussed his plan. "Don't want to leave a mess behind. Sometimes it doesn't matter, but tonight it does. Ashworth was good about being clean, like me, when he needed to. You know, I taught him everything. He took to it right away too. He really loved to inflict pain. I felt I knew that about him the first day I met him. He was with Gary Bell. They showed up at a flophouse trying to arrest some of my whores."

Dennon saw the uncertain look in my eyes.

"I paid off the manager so I could use the top floor as a profitable whorehouse. Right away I sensed Ashworth's and Bell's greed, so all I had to do was offer them a better deal than what LAPD paid. Cops are so easy to manipulate. I showed them a storage closet with a bird's eye view of one of the rooms. The pictures they took of clients who needed to keep their indiscretions secret brought them quite a large chunk of cash. In exchange they left my little enterprise alone. Soon enough they got used to the money and that's when I owned them. The rest is history. They worked to help me build a good business. Make children to sell. It's ingenious. But I didn't do it for the money. I did it for the pleasure." Dennon walked closer toward me. "You've been tracking me and getting closer. You made me kill Gary Bell and those five men. Now you have to go. It could have been different. All you had to do was let Ashworth take the blame for the Belvedere Park murders. If it were up to me, Crowe and McCrudden would be joining you; but they're still invaluable, at least my father thinks so."

Dennon noticed my eyes widen. "You see the resemblance don't you? My father doesn't have my good looks, but I have his blood running through me."

Yes, now I saw it. Bob Dennon was Clay Whitman's son. Gary Bell knew the familial tie and was rightfully afraid.

"When I was thirteen, Father, changed my name and sent me away. He had no other choice. He wasn't about to lose his only son even though I had murdered his daughter, my sister, Roberta. Everyone thought I had died in a fire alongside Roberta, but as you can see I am far from dead. I staged my death so I could get rid of her. I hated her and she had to go. I planned her death for over a year. I pretended to make friends with a boy from a different neighborhood. One day I invited him to play with us at the house. Told him he couldn't tell anyone he was coming over, and if he could pull it off, I'd give him a hundred dollar bill. What a gullible moron; he didn't deserve to live. I locked him in the basement with my sister and set the house on fire."

I didn't know who was more depraved, Bob Dennon or John Ashworth.

"I brought us a nice bottle of champagne for the occasion. Let me pop this open and make a toast before I have to put the gag back in that bleeding mouth of yours."

Dennon walked over to the table to uncork the bottle and pour the champagne and then walked back to me. "I'll free your hands so we can properly toast."

I couldn't believe what I heard. It was my only shot to take him down and I couldn't fail.

Dennon pulled a knife from his pocket and cut through the ropes binding my arms and hands to the chair.

He then handed me a Dixie cup filled with champagne. "I can't risk giving you a glass, but I think you'll still find the taste exquisite even with a paper cup. It's *Perrier-Jouët*, one of the finest champagnes."

Dennon brought his glass up to the light. "I never get bored looking at these bubbles. They're endless."

Dennon stared at his glass for what seemed like an eternity. When he finished he turned his sight back on me and smiled. "You know, I let my guard down with Itzel and got her pregnant. I let her beauty cloud my judgment. Poor thing, she never saw it coming. I think she believed we would be a family."

Dennon lifted his glass in the air. "What shall we toast to?"

I stared in his direction and intentionally avoided his eyes. I dismissed him and he responded with rage.

"Damn you, Alejandra. You can't play along. It would make things a lot easier."

Dennon paused to compose himself. "That's okay. We will toast to me and the business of making and selling children. There really is nothing more profitable when you figure in the minimal investment that's required. Now drink. Drink to me."

I needed to get Dennon closer to me. I brought the cup up to my mouth. I wet my finger in the champagne and ran it across my lips.

"Damn, you're sexy. It's too bad I have to kill you. But until then..."

Dennon pushed into me and pressed his lips over mine. I couldn't give into my disgust. I focused and waited for him to open his mouth. As soon as I felt his lips part I exhaled with all of my force and blew the shard of glass into his throat. Dennon quickly backed away and I saw his eyes roll into his head. From what I could I see I had made the perfect pitch.

Dennon grabbed at his throat and tried to cough up

the shard, but it wouldn't budge. He struggled to breath and then collapsed to the floor. As he moaned and gasped for air his outstretched arm and clenched fist pleaded for help. He appealed to the wrong person. I had no empathy in my soul for this man.

By the time hotel security arrived, Dennon had started to turn blue. He was barely alive and mentally, I was right there with him.

Chapter 23

RECKONING

Several days had passed before Olivia confirmed, using a strand of Dennon's hair and the umbilical cord still attached to the placenta, that Dennon fathered Itzel's missing baby. Olivia's analysis also showed that samples retrieved from the handle of the knife used to kill Itzel matched Dennon's DNA. Even though the results had cleared Crowe, I wasn't convinced he and the Cardinal were free of wrongdoing, but I had nowhere to turn. As for the Cardinal's role, he refused to admit he had been blackmailed into transferring ownership of Archdiocese property to Clay Whitman, and I had no way to determine otherwise. Not even Gary Bell could help me. Gary's death remained undetermined. No evidence at the crime scene could definitively prove he had been murdered or that Bob Dennon was involved. As for Crowe, employees at Angel of Mercy told me the Monsignor dropped off pregnant women before they were ready to give birth. When the women went into labor Dr. Stevens, a physician who offered free medical services to indigent pregnant women, stepped in to help. Angel of Mercy staff identified Bob Dennon as the man who called himself Dr. Stevens and they never questioned the doctor's motives. Dr. Stevens presented his credentials and, given their limited resources, they were happy for the support. By their estimate Dr. Stevens had been called to deliver more than twenty babies from women whom Crowe had dropped off. When I asked about the fate of the mothers and their babies, they had no information to offer.

When news of Dennon's death became public, Ashworth's LAPD accomplices started to talk. Their knowledge of Dennon's enterprise was limited and they had no evidence linking Dennon to any of the crimes. Nevertheless they feared for their lives, believing if they talked to the police Dennon would have found a way to kill them, brutally, like the five murdered men found in the truck bed. They pointed to Ashworth's suicide as proof it was better to kill yourself than give Dennon the pleasure. With the promise of a plea deal, the accomplices told investigators that the plan depended on coaxing Mexican immigrant women into becoming surrogate mothers for a nominal fee. After the children were born the unwitting mothers were murdered and the babies sold to the highest bidder. The accomplices led police back to Ashworth's house where sale transaction records and baby photos were found taped behind a painting of a boat tied alongside a riverbank; the same one I had seen hanging on the wall. Although investigators were not able to determine the whereabouts of all the children, three were rescued.

DNA testing determined that none of the rescued children had been born to Itzel and I wasn't surprised. The more I thought about it the more I couldn't reconcile Dennon selling his own flesh and blood, no matter how sadistic and evil he was. I had a hunch. I called on Captain Allen to help me confirm my suspicion. I knew he would appreciate any chance to make up for his late arrival to the Biltmore Hotel.

§§§§§§§

The gates leading up to the Whitman estate off of Mulholland Drive were closed and locked when we arrived, but an intercom hung on a post off to the side. Captain Allen exited the car and pushed the button. A voice on the other end answered. "Whitman residence."

"Hello. I'm Captain Allen from LAPD. I'd like to speak to Mr. Clay Whitman."

We heard no response to Captain Allen's request. We waited not knowing what to think, but then after a couple of minutes the gates opened. As we slowly drove up the driveway we snaked through lush landscaped grounds filled with Date Palms and Elephant Ears before reaching the expansive two-story mansion. We didn't need to knock on the door. Clay Whitman waited for us outside.

"Hello, Mr. Whitman." I announced.

"Miss Marisol, I had a feeling Captain Allen wasn't traveling alone. Still I didn't think you'd have the nerve to show your face here."

"Why is that, Mr. Whitman? Because in order to save myself I had to kill your son?"

Clay Whitman turned his back toward me and addressed Captain Allen. "I didn't have to let you onto my property, but I did. So what is it you want?"

"Honestly Mr. Whitman, I'm here in an unofficial capacity. My role is to accompany Miss Marisol and make sure she stays safe."

"Well, if that's what's going on you can get back into your car and get the hell off my property."

I interjected, "Mr. Whitman, I have a quick question."

Clay Whitman raised his voice. "Did you not hear me? I said get the hell out of here. And unless you have a warrant, don't you ever come back."

I turned to leave and then stopped when I heard a baby's cry coming from a second floor window. Whitman didn't hesitate to respond. "That baby doesn't concern you."

"But I am concerned, Mr. Whitman. Have you heard of DNA fingerprinting? It's a technique that will prove the baby belongs to your son, Bob Dennon. Or should we call him by his birth name, Robert Whitman?"

"Do you take me for a stupid man?"

"Of course not."

"Good, because I'm way ahead of you. I already know about this so-called DNA evidence that the Coroner submitted to the District Attorney's office. The DA is a friend of mine and I know what's been submitted is not going to be admissible should anyone try to involve me or drag my son, known to have died years ago in a house fire, through the mud. DNA testing has no precedence, plain and simple."

"But you know he never died in that fire. That makes you an accessory."

"That's not how the law will see it. You have nothing. What was it you told me the other day? Men like me won't see it coming and won't be prepared when people like you make a move to take us down. I've been prepared for people like you my whole life. I've seen you coming, Miss Marisol, way before the thought to come after me ever entered your mind." Clay Whitman stepped closer. "This world cannot run without men like me. The system would crumble. You depend on us to breathe and eat. Yes, Miss Marisol, without men like me you don't get to exist."

I held my ground. "You've covered up your son's perversions for a long time. He must have sickened you. He killed your daughter. How do you live with yourself?"

Clay Whitman was done. "You don't understand English. Leave right now before I have you arrested for trespassing and harassment."

I continued. "Don't you give a damn about the children sold by your son? You have a grandchild upstairs; you must feel something."

Whitman turned to address Captain Allen. "If you

don't leave and take this woman with you, I'll make sure your career is finished."

Captain Allen got back in the car and motioned for me to do the same. I sunk into the seat. Whitman had managed to wrestle my spirit free and it was now lying in a puddle at his feet. This battle had been lost. Whitman's power and connections made it so.

We drove away from the property and I didn't know how I'd be able to move forward. Bob Dennon had inflicted unimaginable horror and his death offered no consolation.

From the banked curves of Mulholland Drive I looked down onto a sprawling city with no end in sight. Somewhere on a palm tree lined street there was a child being abused to service someone's pleasure. I had to tolerate this fact; the price for living in this world. But tolerance is very different from acceptance and I wasn't about to accept the brutal pain inflicted by humans. The water of life remains in the dead, but it was also inside of me, hydrating and fortifying my resolve.

"Can you pull over?"

Captain Allen turned into an overlook, a large patch of dirt off the road. I got out of the car and stood to see my city. I reached for my lipstick and removed the cap. I rolled the tube across my mouth and then pressed my lips together to even out the color. Instantly I felt my spirit make its way back home to me. For now Clay Whitman was out of reach, but there were more like him who used their wealth to hide their offenses in the dark. I knew it would be a struggle, but without patience I'd be lost. Like my grandmother, *Nana*, told me, "*La paciencia es como el sol, sin él que no sé este del oeste.*" Patience is like the sun, without it you don't know east from west. I had my sense of direction in check and it was leading me into the shadows. It was there I had to go to shine the light.

Made in the USA
Las Vegas, NV
23 May 2021